BLACK SAXON

The lovely Norman lady Lynette has been forcibly abducted by the mysterious Saxon, Edgar of the Moor, wed in secret and carried off to his home in a remote valley. She swears she will never forgive him. Alone at the manor while Edgar attends the court of Prince Henry, Lynette is subjected to hostility both from Edgar's Saxon people and from his uncle's beautiful young widow Johanna. But why, when she is given the chance, does she refuse to leave the valley?

ALEX ANDREWS

BLACK SAXON

Complete and Unabridged

LINFORD
Leicester

First published in Great Britain in 1982

First Linford Edition
published 1996

British Library CIP Data

Andrews, Alex
    Black Saxon.—Large print ed.—
Linford romance library
    1. English fiction—20th century
    I. Title II. Series
    823.9'14 [F]

ISBN 0-7089-7894-0

Published by
F. A. Thorpe (Publishing) Ltd.
Anstey, Leicestershire

Set by Words & Graphics Ltd.
Anstey, Leicestershire
Printed and bound in Great Britain by
T. J. Press (Padstow) Ltd., Padstow, Cornwall

This book is printed on acid-free paper

1

THE March wind rattled the shutters and made the smoke billow under the rafters of the great hall. Around the central fire dogs prowled among the rushes looking for scraps, while Lynette bent over her embroidery hoping to escape the notice of her irate grandmother. Even the servants had ceased their usual chatter as they brought out the trestles and benches in readiness for supper.

"Eighteen and still unwed!" the lady Gudrun shrieked. "Hugo, how could you bring such disgrace on your own daughter? I grant this manor is hardly the finest dowry a husband could wish for, but to have kept her a maid so long — step forward, girl. Don't hang back there in the shadows."

Lynette laid her work on the bench by the wall and stepped nearer to the light of a guttering torch. Her red-gold hair hung in two long braids and was bound round her forehead with a band of blue wool. A blue tunic clung to firm young breasts and slender waist, girdled with plaited leather that fell in two long thongs down the front of the softly-folding skirt. Because it was still early spring she also wore a mantle of unbleached wool, which though grey and scratchy was warm.

"Lift your head, girl," her grandmother ordered. "Don't slouch like a kitchen wench. Well, your face is pretty enough. Pity you have little else to offer as dowry."

Lynette exchanged a glance with her father. They both knew that he was regarded as a failure and a disgrace to his family.

"I have been trying to explain," he said patiently, "that Lynette is betrothed to Miles of Louth and has been so since she was five years old. If only Miles would come home — "

"Miles of Louth?" Lady Gudrun

interrupted. "Did you say Miles of Louth? Well, well, that is a different matter!"

"You know of him?" Lynette gasped. "Oh, Grandmother, where is he?"

"Where is he? Why, with the king, of course, child! Didn't you know that? God's teeth, see what comes of living among sheep. You don't even know that your betrothed is in high favour at court. I hear the king sends him on errands of state. And he is Sir Miles now. He was knighted."

"That much we had heard," Hugo put in with a wry smile. "Some news does reach this far-flung outpost. But you must be weary. Let me offer you some ale."

"Ale?" The baroness looked down her long nose. "I drink only wine, Hugo. Fortunately, I came prepared." She clapped her hands and from the back of the hall one of her own retainers appeared with a goblet and a skin of wine.

Retreating to her corner bench,

Lynette went on with her sewing, though in the bad light it was difficult and her eyes had begun to ache from the smoke that swirled in the draughts. How she wished that the first flush of spring had not also brought her grandmother to descend on their peaceful lives with her train of servants, her pack-mules and the litter in which she rode slung between two horses.

The old lady, her stringy neck and grey hair concealed by a veil, continued to criticise everything in ringing tones which reached every dim corner of the hall. She said the Braxby servants were slow and slovenly, and when they sat down to supper she declared she could scarcely eat any of the tasteless food. Lynette was thankful that the servants could not understand the Norman French which the family spoke among themselves, though her grandmother's tone and gestures made her feelings clear enough.

"At the castle, there would be venison," she said, turning up her nose at another dish of mutton stew. "We have the hunting rights in our own forest. And our cooks are among the finest in the land. Even the king complimented me on the meals we served when he stayed at the castle."

"The king has visited Cornford?" Hugo asked in surprise.

"Indeed he has — the Conqueror himself, not this wild young Rufus. I have stayed away from the court since Rufus came to the throne, but we hear what passes."

They sat at the high table, across the end of the hall, while two long tables by the walls were used by the servants, whose ranks were swelled by Lady Gudrun's retainers. Hugo's crude armchair had been made in the workshops of the manor, but the lady Gudrun and Lynette perched on stools. Lynette was glad that her father's form hid her from her grandmother, who appeared to have forgotten her existence.

The baroness now launched into tales of court, as she had heard them from travellers and from her oldest son, who as Lord of Cornford owed knight's service to the king and therefore attended the court regularly.

"Yes, things are very different from the Conqueror's time," she told Hugo. "The courtiers have taken to wearing their hair long, like women. They respect nothing, not even the church. Abbots die and the king takes for himself the revenues of their lands."

"Aye, we know," Hugo said gravely. "Our own lord, Abbot Simon, died of a fever last summer and has not yet been replaced. We pay our dues into the king's coffers now."

"Then it is high time this matter of Lynette's marriage was settled. If you should die, and if aught were to happen to Sir Miles, your daughter's future would be in the hands of the king. You must go to court, and have the marriage performed."

"I would prefer it if Sir Miles had

the courtesy to claim his bride himself,"
Hugo said.

"Chaff! I dare say he is too busy
advancing his fortune. You did well
for your daughter there, Hugo."

Turning briefly, Hugo gave Lynette
a smile and squeezed her hand. "I was
fortunate, I dare say. Miles's father has
been our neighbour since we settled
here. Little did we guess that the young
man would rise so high in the world.

Lynette could hardly believe that
the young man she had last seen
six years before was now one of the
king's favourites. She recalled the day,
a bright cold morning in January, when
Miles had ridden by to bid her farewell.
He had been on his way to join
the army which William Rufus was
raising to fight his brother the Duke
of Normandy. Somewhere along the
way, Miles had earned royal favour
and won his spurs.

She pictured him riding a white
charger, like the heroes in the romances
sung by wandering minstrels, a white

cloak flowing behind him and his helmet circled with gold. Miles, so tall, so fair, so handsome — although she had been only twelve years old, she had experienced a warm thrill of pride at the sight of him, though he had scarcely looked at her.

Sometimes at night her body ached for strong arms to hold her and she dreamed of the time when Miles would return to claim her. Hearing her grandmother speak of him only made her more impatient.

"I have passed over thirty years of my life in this land of mists," the baroness was saying as Lynette drifted out of her dreams. "Now I am going home to Normandy. I shall not be sorry to leave these surly Saxon dogs, who hate us."

Glancing up at the servants who hovered, unaware of her grandmother's contempt, Lynette caught the eye of Ralf, the bailiff's son, and smiled at him, making him blush. Poor Ralf. He would miss her when she left Braxby.

"You should be safe in Normandy now," Hugo said.

"Yes," Lady Gudrun sighed. "Duke Robert has gone on Crusade, they say, leaving Rufus as overlord, but at least the fighting is over. Since the Conqueror's death his three sons have done nothing but fight among themselves — Normandy against England, England against Normandy, and young Henry changing sides with every wind that blows. He's a dangerous young whelp, you mark my words. He has even got himself a tame Saxon — a sinister man, if what I hear is true. They say he is a wizard and uses magic spells to keep Prince Henry in his power."

"You cannot believe everything you hear, Mother," Hugo said.

"No, but I saw this Saxon once and I did not like his looks. He wears a wolfskin cloak, like a barbarian, and dresses all in black. From his colouring he is more Celt than Saxon, a man with rough black hair and piercing black eyes." She shuddered with superstitious fear, but Lynette listened in fascination.

"He swims like a fish, too," her grandmother went on. "They say he saved Prince Henry's life when the prince's horse floundered at a river crossing. The prince knighted him — a Saxon, mind! But where he came from no one knows. They say he was raised in the forest by wolves, and may be a Saxon prince only waiting his moment to raise a rebellion."

"What nonsense!" Hugo exclaimed with a laugh. "This is women's gossip, Mother."

"Not so," she replied. "Your brother Tancred has told me there are those at court who mistrust this Saxon. His greatest enemy is Miles of Louth, who has been heard to vow that if the Saxon gives him the least cause he will cut him down, for the safety of the whole realm."

"Can one man be so dangerous?" Hugo asked, and yawned hugely. "It grows late, Mother. Let us sleep, and hope the Saxon hordes do not descend during the night."

Cursing him for a light-minded fool, Lady Gudrun ceased her baleful chatter.

Later, Lynette lay in her sleeping chamber behind the curtain at the end of the hall, listening as her grandmother snored on the other side of the wooden partition. Hugo had given up his private bed-chamber for his mother's sake and was bedded down in the great hall with the rest of the household.

Lynette loved her father, but his lack of ambition irked her and she could understand why her grandmother was so impatient with him. He was the youngest of the three sons of Baron Cornford, who had won his lands fighting for the Conqueror. Hugo's oldest brother had inherited the lands and title; his middle brother had become a monk; and Hugo had gone to be a household knight, fighting for his patron in return for his keep, though he had never enjoyed the life as some did.

In London he had met the rich young widow of a merchant, married her and with her money bought the manor of Braxby. But if anyone suspected that Hugo had married solely for wealth he would be wrong, Lynette thought. She well remembered the love that had flowed between her parents, warming her and making her secure, and when her mother had died her father had been inconsolable for many months.

But if Hugo enjoyed the quiet life of the country, Lynette often found herself bored. It might have been different if she had been wed, with children to care for, but acting as mistress of Braxby was unsatisfying. She longed to see something of the world, for she had never been further than the tiny settlement of Louth, which held the nearest market. Tales of the outside made her itch with curiosity to see for herself.

And now she learned that her

betrothed was an important man. With him she could travel, visiting the manors he must have been given as rewards for his services. She might even go to court and see the king and his brother the prince, together with all the great lords and ladies of the realm. And how she would love to see the black Saxon knight! Filled with excitement, she dreamed happy dreams.

Stirrings in the hall outside woke her as the dawn light seeped in between the window shutters. She leapt out of bed to splash cold water on her face and dress hurriedly.

In the hall the fire had been lit. Ralf the bailiff's son was opening the shutters to let in more light and cold air through the narrow window openings, while others cleared away their pallets and thin blankets, breaking their fast hastily before hurrying off to other tasks.

Ralf brought Lynette her portion of grey bread and fresh-brewed ale frothing in a horn mug. The two usually ate breakfast together in a corner of the hall, for the first food of the day was not taken formally at table.

"The wind has dropped," Ralf said in the Saxon English which Lynette spoke as well as French. He seated himself on the bench beside her. "They'll be able to get on with the sowing today."

"Yes." That morning she was not interested in the hum-drum routine of the manor and scarcely noticed Ralf. While she gazed at his round, open face with its rough-cropped brown hair she was seeing the handsome Miles, golden-fair as a Viking with eyes like speedwells. The picture was not clear, for she could hardly remember what Miles really looked like, not after six years, but she had built an image of him in her mind and clung to it more fondly now she had news of him.

"We shall be going to court, Ralf," she said, her green eyes shining. "My grandmother says that Sir Miles is one of the king's most trusted knights. My father will take me to him and we shall be wed."

"Aye," Ralf said softly.

Lynette watched as one of her grandmother's servants carried a platter of bread and a goblet of watered wine into the sleeping chamber, and when she looked again at Ralf she saw the sadness in him and was sorry her thoughts had been elsewhere.

"But you needn't worry," she said with a smile. "My father will go on with the lessons, if you ask him. You really ought to learn French, Ralf, if you want to rise in the world."

"Learning won't be much use to me," Ralf said. "As to rising in the world — that's not for the likes of me. No doubt I'll be bailiff here after my father, and my son after me."

A gleam of mischief danced in her eyes. "Your son? Have you chosen a wife, then? Who is she, Ralf? Young Mildgyth, the shepherd's daughter?"

"Maybe," Ralf said, flushing. "Since

I cannot wed you, I'll make do with Mildgyth."

Lynette stared at him, shocked by the very idea of his marrying her. They had been almost as close as brother and sister all their lives, but until now neither had forgotten for an instant that their stations were very different.

"I was jesting," Ralf mumbled, and took himself away.

Feeling disturbed by his strange remark, Lynette waited impatiently for her grandmother to appear, intending to ask questions about Miles and the court, but when the baroness emerged from behind the curtain she was in a hurry to be on her way.

"Already, Grandmother?" Lynette said in dismay. "I hoped you would stay a few days with us."

"I might have done," Lady Gudrun retorted, "if my son had not chosen to live in a pig-sty among uncouth Saxon peasants. No, my child, I must be moving on. I have a long journey ahead of me. But I am glad to have seen you. Be sure your father sees to it that you are wed before long."

"Yes, Grandmother."

"And lift your head! Be proud! You are a Norman." She looked Lynette up and down hopelessly. "You must have some new clothes, too. You don't want Sir Miles to be ashamed of you, do you? God's blood, I can still scarce believe it. Eighteen! When I was your age I had been wed four years and borne two children. It's a pity I must leave before we get this settled, but perhaps I may find some way of helping you. I expect news very soon. Do you hear me?"

"Yes, Grandmother."

The brief visit unsettled Lynette and as spring laid its green veil over the trees she longed to see Miles and become his wife. Her father sent word to Miles's parents, who replied that they had sent many messages but always the answer came that Miles was too busy to return home. He would come when the king gave him leave.

His parents were embarrassed by his long absence and Lynette knew her father was troubled, too.

She went about her duties as mistress of the household with rising impatience, for now that she had seen the manor through her grandmother's eyes she began to feel even more dissatisfied.

As the weather turned warmer, she rode out with Ralf most afternoons to look over the sheep. She rode astride, not caring that it was considered unladylike, for she enjoyed the freedom of being about the manor. She and Ralf would pause at the cottages of wattle and daub to enquire after a new baby or someone who was sick, while all around them the villagers went about their work, tending the cultivated strips in the fields.

These outings to look at the sheep began to depress Lynette, for almost every time they would encounter young Mildgyth on her way to take bread and cheese to her shepherd father, so Lynette was obliged to witness the burgeoning romance between Ralf and the slender girl. It only served to remind her more sharply of Miles's absence.

Worse still was the suspicion that he might have grown too grand for her. He might consider her unworthy now to be his wife, and if that happened she would be forced to face the prospect of a nunnery. No other young man had ever shown interest in her. But when these thoughts came to her she thrust them to the back of her mind, telling herself that of course Miles would honour his betrothal promises. He was too chivalrous to cast her aside.

Sometimes she felt she hated the wooded hills which bordered the manor and shut her off from everything that was of interest. Everything in the valley was so familiar — the water-mill; the little wooden church; the pigs that rooted and the dogs that roamed. And when she rode through the gate into the courtyard she felt imprisoned by the thorn hedge and the jumble of rude outhouses, barns, kitchen huts and stables. Often she sent a silent scream up to heaven. When would Miles come? She longed to know the joy of being held in his arms.

On a mild April day when rain washed the hills, a party of pilgrims arrived to beg shelter for the night. Lynette listened eagerly to their tales of London and an escape from robbers in the thick forests along the way, but most of all she was thrilled to hear that the king was coming north and planned to be in Lincoln for St George's Day.

At supper, while the torches smoked and the servants chattered, she told her father the news.

"We must go!" she added. "Miles will be there. Father, since he cannot come to me I must go to him. It is my duty."

Hugo frowned. "I wonder, sometimes, if it is that he cannot come, or that he will not come."

"He cannot," she said at once, disturbed to hear him voice her own doubts. "The king needs him. Father, two days' journey is not beyond our means. Ralf would go with us. He is sturdy, should there be outlaws beside the road. Please, Father!"

"I shall think on it," Hugo said, and was wracked by the cough which had troubled him for several days.

Concerned for him, Lynette said no more about journeying to the county town, but she determined to go, one way or another.

It seemed that fate was equally determined to deny her, for her father's cough grew worse during the next few days and despite herbal remedies and spells muttered by an old woman of the village he sank into a fever. Clearly he would be unfit to travel, and there were only two more days before the feast of St George.

Lynette paced the hall in a fever of impatience, torn between anxiety for her father and her need to seek Miles. When she heard Hugo call she hurried into the sleeping chamber and found him lying on his bed, sweat beading his pale brow. Beside him, looking grave, stood the bailiff Cerdic and his son Ralf.

Hugo held out a shaking hand and she took it between her own, sinking to the floor beside him.

"We have been discussing the matter of your marriage," he told her, breath rasping in his lungs. "It must be settled at once. I fear I delayed through selfishness, my love. I did not want you to leave me. But if I die you will be alone. You must find Miles. I see that now. Go to Lincoln — Ralf will go with you and protect you."

That was what she had longed to hear, but on seeing how ill her father was her resolve weakened. "How can I leave you? You need my care, Father."

"You must not think of me," Hugo croaked. "Old Agnes will tend me. And if my time has come then I shall be happier knowing your future is settled. For my sake, my love, you must find Miles. You could be wed at once. It would not do for you to be left here alone, still a maid."

Lynette saw that he meant what he said, so she forbore to argue, but it was not the way she had planned to go — not leaving behind a sick man who might die while she was away. Even the joy of being married at last to Miles could not make her forgive herself if something should happen to her father. And suppose Miles did not want her?

With a heavy heart she prepared for the journey, bundling a few changes of clothes and some food for the journey into a pack which would be carried by a mule. The following morning she bade farewell to her father, not knowing if she would ever see him again.

Since they were leaving the confines of the valley she was obliged to follow convention and ride uncomfortably, pillion behind Ralf, with the mule behind on a leading rein. As they came to the crest of the hill she looked back at the valley, suddenly loath to leave it.

How dear and comfortable it seemed, nestled among its hills.

"I shall come back," she said, almost to herself.

"Aye, mistress, you will," Ralf replied.

At that moment the rain swept down and she bent her head inside the hooded cloak that was lined with sheepskin, while tears trickled down her face. Ralf's sturdy back gave her some protection from the weather, but nothing could soothe the ache in her heart and the fears that beset her.

They travelled all day, sometimes walking to rest the horse, pausing once near midday to eat the cold food they had brought and to drink from a stream. Sunset found them on the edges of a manor, where a steward greeted them and gave them food and lodging for the night.

At dawn they set out again in company with two peasants leading donkeys to market in Lincoln. The animals bore panniers woven of rushes which contained plants picked in the woods — woad for dyeing, herbs for medicines, oak-galls and blackthorn roots for making ink. Lynette had begun to regain some of her excitement, for it was St George's Day and Miles should be in Lincoln. Perhaps she would see him before nightfall.

Jogging along with a hand tucked in Ralf's belt, she allowed herself to indulge in her favourite dream. She saw Miles running down steps into a castle courtyard, to kneel before her and vow his undying love, his blue eyes shining as he begged her to forgive him for his long absence. And when they were alone he would take her in his arms and . . .

The dream stopped abruptly as the loud barking of dogs and the faint sound of a hunting horn came on the breeze. Lynette saw that they were surrounded by deep gladed woods where tiny leaves unfurled in the sunlight. She saw a vague red shape come crashing through the trees and a stag dashed out across the track to plunge into the woods on the far side, the hunt hallooing not far behind.

Ralf slid from the grey mare to hold it more steady as the hunting dogs flitted through the dappled shade towards them, but before he had firm hold of the reins the lead hound came baying right under the mare's nose. The horse bolted, while Lynette clung grimly to the saddle amid a confusion of dogs that raced across her path.

She lunged for the reins, but missed them and lay helplessly clinging to the horse's mane. Then her seat slipped and for a wild moment she tossed against the mare's flank until her fingers loosed their grip on the saddle and she tumbled inelegantly, rolling into the wet grass.

Some distance behind her, the hunt streamed across the track, horsemen and dogs, huntsmen afoot blowing horns, but she was almost too stunned to notice. She lay breathless, bewildered, only vaguely aware of galloping hoofbeats coming nearer.

From her eye corner she saw the legs of a huge black charger stop beside her as its rider jumped lightly to the ground. He wore leather boots, black stockings thonged with leather, a short black tunic slit at the sides, and a black cloak that swirled heavily with its lining of rough grey fur.

"Are you hurt?" a deep voice asked in pure Norman French as the man bent beside her, a hand on her shoulder.

"I think not, thank you, sir," she murmured, her face hot with shame. "I was — winded for a moment."

She found herself staring into a strong brown face with a stern mouth. Unruly black hair tumbled over eyes as dark as the inside of a cave, eyes that held her spellbound until he broke the spell by glancing down at her tumbled clothes. Lynette reached to pull down the tunic which had ridden up to display her stockinged legs, though thank heaven her bare thighs remained covered. Shaking off her faintness she managed, with his help, to stand up.

Aches and pains stung every part of her, but there seemed to be no real damage, except that she would be bruised. She realised suddenly that she was still leaning against the stranger, his strong arm round her waist. She eased away, murmuring embarrassed thanks.

"Prince Henry will be sorry that his morning's hunting caused you harm," her rescuer said.

She stared up at the brown face, startled and dismayed. "Prince Henry? He hunts alone? Is the king not come to Lincoln — the king and all his court?"

"The king and all who travel with him," the man agreed, a glint of amusement in his black eyes, "and some who come to pursue their business affairs. Are you anxious to see the glitter of the court, my lady?"

Lynette realised she was being made the object of his fun and, remembering her grandmother's advice, she straightened herself, tilting her chin proudly to stare her rescuer in the eye.

"No, sir. I am on my way to see my betrothed, who is with the court."

"A fortunate man, indeed," he said, teasing her with his look. "Perhaps I know him. May I enquire his name?"

"Sir Miles of Louth," Lynette said.

She was surprised by the frown that suddenly darkened his face and wiped the smile from his eyes.

"Indeed?" he muttered. "I do know Sir Miles. And you are his betrothed? Where do you come from?"

"From Braxby, sir. I doubt you will know it. It is only a small manor, not many miles from Louth."

The fury grew in him until she felt that his eyes were made of black fire, searing into her, but she could not look away.

"I shall tell Sir Miles you are on your way," he said tautly. "Good day, my lady."

He swung away, the edge of his cloak brushing against her as he set foot in the stirrup and leapt with easy grace to the saddle. From there he regarded her upturned face, his white teeth showing in a humourless smile. "You might tell Sir Miles, if you see him first, that you were aided by Edgar of the Moor. I doubt it will please him, but tell him all the same."

Touching spur to his mount, he was away, galloping in under the trees with his cloak flying to display its grey fur lining. Still breathless, Lynette watched him for a moment, and jumped when Ralf spoke from behind her.

"Who is that man?"

Lynette saw that he had rescued her horse for her. She had been so intrigued by the other man that she had forgotten Ralf, but now she saw him scowling after the retreating horseman.

"He said his name was Edgar of the Moor." She repeated it to herself — Edgar of the Moor. It had a strange, wild ring to it that she found exciting.

"A Saxon name," Ralf said. "But I like him not, mistress. I trust no man who wears wolfskin."

"Wolfskin?" Lynette echoed, and stared into the woods where her rescuer had disappeared, her heart jolting. If she had not been so dazed she might have realised before — a man who rode with Prince Henry, dressed all in black and wearing a cloak lined with wolfskin. He must be the black Saxon knight of whom her grandmother had spoken!

The next second she recalled something else her grandmother had said — the Saxon knight was Miles's deadly enemy.

2

THE slowness of their pace made Lynette's impatience rise. She kept worrying about her sick father, left at home, and the nearer she approached to the town the more uncertain she grew about her meeting with Miles. She thought, too, about the dark-faced Edgar of the Moor, little ripples of nervous excitement running up and down her spine. Saxon prince or sinister wizard — whichever he was, he had been kind to her.

When the sun began to sink from its highest point, shining full in her eyes, Lynette heard the sound of great celebrations ahead. Trumpets blared and many voices called and chattered, amid much laughter and some clashing of weapons. As the small party emerged from the woods they came upon a stretch of open ground where a fair was in progress.

Lynette glimpsed the stalls of traders among a throng of people and elsewhere more crowds gathered to watch sports — wrestling in one place, a bear being baited in another. She heard the low growls of the animal and the yapping of the dogs that tormented it, and she felt sick at the cruelty. Once a dancing bear had come with its owner to Braxby and she had stroked its fur, finding it a gentle beast. That men should find pleasure in inflicting pain this way distressed her.

The crowds jostled on all sides, forcing the horse to slow its pace further, but beyond the crush of people and flying pennants Lynette saw the walls of the town, with the tower of the cathedral church rising towards the sky, and the castle keep beyond it. She began to understand the difficulty of the quest she had undertaken, for Miles could be anywhere in the crowd, or perhaps on duty at the castle.

"Mistress, see," Ralf said, drawing

her attention to the tournament lists where yet more people had gathered as spectators.

In the centre of the circle, a small group of gorgeously-dressed men, glinting with gold and jewels, stood by a dais where another man, corpulent and with yellow hair, slouched in a chair. In front of him, on a carpet spread on the grass, knelt a young man dressed in white tunic and leather jerkin sewn with metal rings. Around him attendants bore his lance and shield, while to a blare of trumpets a sword was carried in with ceremony.

"A knighting!" Lynette breathed to Ralf, glad that from her perch on the horse she had a good view. The man on the dais, she realised with a jolt of excitement, must be the king himself, and Miles might not be far from him. Scanning the group around the king, she sought eagerly for a glimpse of her betrothed.

Above the noise of the crowd it was impossible to hear the words of the oath as the king stood up to remind the candidate of his duties as a knight, and the young man, kneeling, made his vow. Then the king helped him to his feet, embraced him, and with another fanfare the war-horse was led into the arena in full harness. Amid great cheers the new knight mounted, took up lance and shield, and spurred his horse to a gallop to show himself to the crowd.

Lynette was disappointed by the sight of the king. He was excessively fat, red-faced, and his yellow hair looked like straw. He was not even very tall.

"We had best go on," she said to Ralf. "We must find lodgings."

But as Ralf urged the horse into a walk the trumpets called again and another knight dressed for war rode into the arena. His blue cloak tossed in the breeze and the nose-piece of his helmet obscured his face, but the cry went up, "Sir Miles! Sir Miles!" The name spread through the crowd until all the noisy onlookers, many of them drunk, were shouting it."

Lynette clutched Ralf's arm, said, "Wait!" and watched breathlessly as the two knights faced each other with lances held at the ready. The weapons were tipped with wooden crowns, so that no real harm could be done, but even so Lynette knew that broken, bones often resulted from such display fights.

While the crowd roared them on, the two horsemen rode at each other, a crash resounding as each lance met a shield. Both men shuddered under the impact, but the horses plunged on and swung round to face each other again. Twice more the blow of their meeting cracked through the air, and the second time the new knight toppled from his saddle. As he sprawled on the ground his squire ran to help him up. The crowd cheered anew as Miles rode proudly round the ring.

Someone close to Lynette said, "'Tis no shame to be bested by the king's champion. The young man made a brave show."

She found that her heart was beating unsteadily as the blue-cloaked figure came nearer. Somehow Ralf had edged their horse to the front of the crowd and for a second Lynette looked directly into Miles's blue eyes. How broad he had grown. How strong and fine. Her own knight!

He stared straight through her and rode on. Dismayed, Lynette watched the blue cloak swirl across his horse's flank, and tears pricked behind her eyes. Miles had not recognised her, had scarcely even seen her.

"His mind was elsewhere," Ralf said swiftly. "He did not expect to see you here; mistress. And six years have changed you."

Six years had changed Miles, too, Lynette thought. He had been a stripling of seventeen when last she saw him, riding off to his first battle. Now he was the king's champion, known to all. Suddenly she was aware of her dusty, travel-weary state, her tunic torn and muddied from her earlier fall, dyed dark blue from the woad that was cheapest of all dyes. Small wonder that Miles had not come to claim her. She was unworthy of him.

"Ride on," she ordered. "We must find a place to rest for the night."

She huddled miserably behind Ralf, her hood drawn round her face although the sun shone warmly. She felt that everyone in that great crowd must have noticed her humiliation and she only wished she had remained at Braxby, with her dreams intact.

The noise of the fair had begun to dwindle behind them when she felt Ralf stiffen. She looked up, to see the gates of the town not far away. A few people around her were also leaving the fair, laughing as they recounted sights they had seen, but what drew Lynette's eyes was the tall black horse and rider who were approaching from the town. Even before she made out his face she knew from his black garb that it was Edgar of the Moor. The people edged away to avoid him, some of them crossing themselves as if for protection against evil.

From the taut set of Ralf's body she guessed that his face would be stony. He, too, feared the dark knight, though he was Saxon himself. But Lynette remembered laughter in black eyes and was sure that Edgar was a mere mortal, not a wizard to be feared.

Ralf would have ridden by, but Edgar set his horse in their path, drawing rein as they came near. Ralf was obliged to halt.

"I trust your lady has taken no harm from her fall," Edgar said, using Saxon English that was differently accented from the Lincolnshire variety.

"She was shaken, my lord," Ralf replied.

Speculative dark eyes met Lynette's as she peered out from her hood, hoping that he would not see the traces of tears on her face.

"Are you seeking lodgings, my lady?" he asked.

She wished he would not insist on

calling her 'my lady', for it was obviously a taunt. "We are," she replied. "We would be on our way were we not obstructed."

"My apologies." He spoke gravely, but the demon of laughter was back in his eyes as he drew aside, turning his horse so that he rode beside Lynette, tall on his great black charger. "If you will allow me to accompany you, my lady, I shall gladly direct you to the Abbey. The Abbot is a friend of mine. He will give you rooms."

Grateful as she was for this offer of help in a strange town; she was too depressed to do more than say, "Thank you, sir."

"It is my pleasure," he assured her. "No gentleman could allow the betrothed lady of Sir Miles of Louth to go unescorted. What were your parents thinking of?"

Aware that she was being baited, Lynette opened her mouth to say something sharp, but the memory of her sick father made her pause.

"My mother is dead and my father very sick," she replied. "That is why I come to find Sir Miles, though I wish now that I had stayed at home."

A dark eyebrow lifted behind the shaggy hair on his forehead. "Having come so far? But Sir Miles will be delighted to see you."

Lynette almost blurted out that she had already seen Miles and, far from being delighted, he had not even noticed her. But she closed her lips on the words of bitterness and bent her head.

"I shall myself make sure that he is advised of your arrival," Edgar of the Moor said.

They came into the streets of the city, narrow lanes close-set with wooden houses and shops, dogs wandering in the garbage that littered the central drain. It smelled like the midden at Braxby, Lynette thought, drawing her cloak round her nose.

Eventually they approached the walls

of the Abbey and Edgar spoke to the gatekeeper. The courtyard was busy with people — monks and merchants, men-at-arms and servants — most of them were travelling with the court.

A short while later, Lynette found herself in a small chamber furnished with a narrow bed and a stool. One of the Abbey servants brought her water and she washed away the stains of travel, shivering in the cold evening air as the sun went down. In the garden beyond the arched window opening, birds flitted among the budding trees and yellow daffodils nodded.

Puzzled thoughts about Edgar of the Moor filled her mind as she dressed in clean clothes. She did not understand him. He had promised to tell Miles she was staying at the Abbey, but with him there was that underlying tone of mockery. She could not forget what her grandmother had said about the Saxon knight: "Sir Miles has vowed to kill him."

Since she hoped to see Miles, she put

on her best over-tunic of bright yellow embroidered with flowers round the flowing hem and bell-shaped sleeves. She re-braided her long hair, threading it with green ribbons, and completed her outfit with a long mantle of brown wool edged with rabbit fur.

She ate supper in the Abbot's hall, along with all the other guests, including Ralf, who sat below the salt. When they had eaten they were entertained by minstrels and tumblers, but Lynette found herself unable to enjoy the spectacle. It was well after sunset and still Miles had not come. Soon curfew would ring.

As she slipped away from the hall, Ralf joined her, a gloomy look on his face.

"If there is anything I can do, mistress — "

"What can anyone do but wait?" Lynette replied wearily. "I have come this far. The rest is up to Sir Miles. But if he does not come, Ralf, I shall be tempted to go to the castle and demand to see him. How much longer must I wait for him?"

"Perhaps Sir Edgar has not told him you are here," Ralf said with a frown. "I don't trust that man, mistress. There's mischief in his look. I've been talking to some of the others who share my quarters and they say that Edgar of the Moor is a warlock."

"But you have seen him!" Lynette replied impatiently. "He is human, just as you and I are."

"Aye, but they say that even the king mistrusts him, and that he is the sworn enemy of Sir Miles. If that's true, why did he act so kindly to you? I fear he may have some evil plan in mind."

"Oh, what could he possibly do?" Lynette cried. "Ralf — I'm very tired. In the morning we will decide what must be done. Go now and sleep."

Before Ralf could reply, a monk came hurrying along the shadowed walk, his black habit swishing round his feet.

"My lady?" he said. "Are you the

lady Lynette of Braxby?"

"I am."

In the faint light the monk's smile showed pale beneath his hood. "I am pleased to have found you. My lady, I beg you come with me. Sir Miles of Louth awaits you."

Lynette caught her breath, unable to speak for a spurt of joy that was mingled with apprehension. She clutched Ralf's hand briefly, sensing the bleakness of his feelings, and turned to follow the monk.

Through passageways and up stairs, with thudding heart she stepped after her guide, coming at last to a door where the monk bowed and left her. Lynette laid a hand on the wooden latch, took a deep breath and lifted her head high as she stepped inside the room.

For a few silent moments she stared at the tall figure of her betrothed. This was a meeting she had dreamed of, but now that it had come she was afraid. Candlelight shone gold in his fair hair and caught on a scar across his cheek, but he was the most handsome man she had ever seen — apart, perhaps, from Edgar of the Moor.

How was he looking at her? she wondered. Did she look well, or could he see that she was only the daughter of a poor country knight? With relief she saw him smile warmly, still the Miles she remembered even though he had matured.

"My lady!" he said softly, taking two swift strides to kneel before her, lifting her hand to his lips.

Lynette discovered she was trembling, torn with feelings she did not understand. "Please — do not kneel to me, Miles. You are the king's champion and I — "

"You are the lady of my heart," he said fervently, gazing up at her with intense blue eyes. "How beautiful you have grown. Had I known, nothing would have kept me from your side."

"You might have known sooner, if you had come home," she said, unable to resist the mild reproof.

Miles came to his feet, holding her hand to his breast. "Forgive me. I would have come, but the king is my master and I must go where he sends me. I have scarce been in one place for a full week together, in all these long years. And the king — as you know, he is unmarried himself — he does not take the feelings of his servants into account."

"You are not angry that I came?" she asked.

"Angry?" He kissed her hand again, pain in his blue eyes. "How could I be angry when you stand before me at last, so beautiful and tender? My love, if I were master of my own life we would be married this night."

She stared up at him in the candlelight, fighting a sense of unreality. Though she had dreamed fond dreams of him, Miles in the flesh was a stranger. The thought of being wed to a shining dream knight was one thing, but to think of herself as wife to this strong, muscular man brought blood rushing to her face.

"I did not come to rush you into marriage," she said. "But my father is ill, Miles. He was afraid that I might be left unprotected."

"Then return to him," Miles replied. "Set his fears at rest. I swear to you I shall come to Braxby before harvest-time and make you my bride. Having seen you, I shall be impatient for the day. I will beg leave of the king and ride to you on swift wings of love."

"But I could stay a few days here," Lynette said. "We could meet, and — "

"How I wish it could be so," he sighed. "But I must leave tomorrow. The king commands me away on an important mission. You must understand, my love, that a knight must follow his lord's orders. I am not free to go where I please. If I were, I would not be parted from you for a single minute, I swear."

Her wide green eyes fixed on his face anxiously. "Then — then I shall not see you until you come for me?"

"Alas, no. It is a great sorrow to me, too. But make yourself busy preparing for me. I must go now, before curfew is rung. Come, I'll take you to the courtyard."

A few minutes later, Lynette was alone in the dark cloisters, her hand still burning from Miles's last kiss and her heart desolate. The meeting had been so brief, so rushed, and he had not even attempted to take her in his arms or kiss her mouth. Perhaps that was honourable, but her lips ached for the caress he had not bestowed and she was suddenly filled with panic. Before the summer was out she would be the wife of a man she hardly knew, sharing his home — and his bed.

She hardly slept that night, despite her tiredness, but lay watching the moonlight creep across her tiny chamber as she forced herself to accept her fate. Marriage, after all, was a business arrangement rather than a romantic binding of two hearts. She was more fortunate than many women, for Miles was young, handsome, healthy and in high favour at court. As his wife, Lynette saw herself becoming mistress of castles and manors, mother of the heir to those lands. There would be wealth and plenty.

Why, then, did she long for something more — something she could not define? Its absence laid a cold band round her heart and when at last she fell asleep there were tears on her cheeks.

The morning sunlight raised her spirits, however. Miles was busy, that was all. When the time came they would both have an opportunity to learn about love together. 'I am betrothed to the king's own champion,' she thought, and as she and Ralf rode forth from the town to begin the long journey home she held her head high, as her grandmother had taught her.

They were accompanied at first by peasants on foot going home after the St George's Day festivities, but gradually these companions drifted away as they came near the scattered manors. By mid afternoon Lynette and Ralf were alone, travelling through deep woods with the mule trailing behind.

"We should have waited for someone who was going nearer to Braxby," Ralf said. "I heard tales of a band of robbers roaming these woods."

"Why should robbers bother with us?" Lynette replied. "We have nothing of value."

"We've got the horse, and the mule. I wish we had waited."

"We could not wait!" she said sharply. "I have been away from my father for long enough. I want to be at home to care for him. Besides, Ralf, we saw no sign of robbers on our journey from Braxby; You have let yourself be frightened by idle gossip."

"It was not idle gossip," Ralf argued. "I spoke to a man who had been attacked himself, and robbed of everything he possessed — including his clothes."

"Nonsense!" Lynette was disturbed,

in spite of her show of bravado. "If you cannot be cheerful, then be silent."

He pulled the horse to a halt, slid from the saddle and mumbled that he would lead it for a while, to relieve the animal of his weight, though Lynette knew that his real reason was a desire to escape from her nearness. Ever since her meeting with Miles, Ralf had been surly with her.

"In that case," she said, swinging her leg across the saddle, "I shall ride comfortably for a while."

What a relief it was to be solidly astride the horse instead of perched behind the saddle in constant danger of sliding off!

Ralf gave her a baleful look. "A fine thing for the future wife of the king's champion."

"Mind your manners!" Lynette snapped.

"Oh, yes, my lady. Your pardon, my lady."

"Ralf!"

Unabashed, he stared her in the

eye, his face red. "When we return to Braxby, I shall ask the priest to marry me and Mildgyth at once."

"You may do as you please," Lynette returned. "I hope it will improve your temper."

Ralf turned his face to the front and plodded for a while in silence. Eventually he glanced round and said with a sigh, "Forgive me, mistress. I'm worried about you, that's all. We've always been friends, haven't we?"

"And always shall be," Lynette added. "Friends, Ralf."

"I meant nothing more," he said swiftly, colour staining his cheeks. "But a friend — even a man like me — could worry about you, couldn't he?"

"Worry?" Lynette repeated, puzzled. "About what?"

"About — " He hesitated, his face twisting. "At the Abbey, they were saying things about — "

He broke off as the sound of galloping hooves came pounding behind them along the grassy track. Ralf stopped the horse, the reins tightly in one hand while with the other he took from his belt the stout-stick he carried for defence.

Twisting round in the saddle, Lynette saw a horseman emerge from the cover of the trees, his dark cloak flowing behind him as he rode at full gallop after them. One glance was enough to tell her the identity of that black-clad man and she watched in disquiet as he came level, sawing at the reins so that his horse reared briefly before settling to the ground.

"Well met, my lady," Edgar of the Moor said with a slight smile.

Ralf had put himself between them, the stick ready as his freckled face set in a frown. "I must ask you your business, sir."

"My business?" Edgar repeated, his smile widening. "Why, my good fellow, as a true knight my business is, among other things, protecting fair ladies. Put down your cudgel, man. I offer help, not harm."

"On your honour as a knight?" Ralf demanded.

"On my honour as a Saxon warrior," Edgar said gravely, then smiled as he added, "And as a servant of Prince Henry. I admire your courage, fellow, but I could cut you in two if I chose. Were my intentions evil you would not be still on your feet threatening me."

Lynette leaned down to touch Ralf's shoulder. "Put down your stick, Ralf. Sir Edgar knows full well what Sir Miles would do to him if he should harm me. I think we are safe enough."

"Aye," Edgar said softly, his eyes narrowing. "The thought of Sir Miles of Louth sends terror through me indeed."

Thrusting the cudgel back in his belt, Ralf turned to lead the horse on, muttering under his breath, "I don't like it."

Lynette was not happy with the situation, either. It appeared that Edgar had come chasing after them solely to inflict his company on them, but what reasons had prompted him? He had no love for Miles. Why should he put himself out to protect Miles's future bride?

"You saw Sir Miles, I gather," he said, riding alongside her.

"I did, sir. I owe you my thanks for arranging it."

"Did Sir Miles tell you I arranged it?"

"He did not mention your name, and neither did I. We had more important issues to discuss. But since you promised to inform him of my presence — "

"I made sure he had the message," Edgar interrupted. "Though for discretion's sake I forebore to let him know from whence it came. Sir Miles is a suspicious fellow — like your servant here."

"From what I hear," Lynette said boldly, "they are not the only two who mistrust you."

His smile was cold and left his eyes unfathomable. "I have heard that, too, my lady. But mistrust is a sickness which touches all in an unsettled land."

"No longer unsettled, sir, since the king put down the rebellions and made peace with his brother in Normandy."

"A land is bound to be unsettled when oppressors sit on the necks of good honest men," Edgar said.

"The Normans are not oppressors!" Lynette replied sharply. "Your own king Edward named the Conqueror as his successor."

"And thereby disinherited his own nephew," Edgar added.

"Who was a child, at the time, and has been only too happy to accept Norman friendship. Does he not spend much of his time with the court? Oh, yes, sir, even in Braxby we hear the news."

Edgar's mouth stretched again in a thin smile. "Let us not argue politics, my lady. You are Norman and I am Saxon, but our peoples are striving to find harmony. Perhaps we two can do our part."

"As to that," Lynette retorted, tilting her chin, "I shall thank you for your protection, sir — when we reach the gates of Braxby safely."

As the sun sank low behind them they came to a stream tumbling down a wooded hillside, where they stopped to drink the cold, clear water. Under Edgar's sardonic gaze, Ralf helped Lynette to dismount and she stretched her aching legs and back, walking briskly beneath the trees before bending to take some water in the cup which hung on her girdle.

She sat down on the grass, letting the water trickle down her dry throat, soothing and refreshing her, while she watched the clouds chase across the sky. A hawk sailed effortlessly on the air currents and the woods were full of long shadows and rays of golden light.

"We seem to have missed our way," Ralf murmured, kneeling beside Lynette to catch some water in his own cup. "By now we should have sighted the manor where we stayed two nights ago. This Sir Edgar is misleading us."

Lynette glanced along the bank to where Edgar stood not three strides away, his black cloak around him and his dark hair lifting on the breeze. "You have been leading us, not he," she argued. "We must have passed the manor by now."

"And if we do not find another, nightfall will come on us while we are out in the open," Ralf replied. "You should have sent this knight away, mistress. I don't trust him."

"So you keep saying!" she said irritably.

She realised that Edgar was watching them, clearly wondering what they were whispering about, so she stood up, shaking out her skirts and resettling her heavy cloak.

"Your Lincolnshire water is sweet," Edgar remarked. "As refreshing as the wines of France."

"We thrive on it," Lynette said. "Sir Edgar, we must seek shelter for the night. The villages are scattered among these hills and your horse is faster than mine. Will you ride ahead and see if we are within reach of a settlement?"

"Send your servant," he replied. "He may borrow my horse, if he thinks he can ride it."

"I can ride anything on four legs!" Ralf stated, scrambling to his feet. "But if you think I'll leave my lady alone with you, you can — "

The words broke off as a stick cracked in the woods. Ralf whirled and Edgar reached out to grab Lynette, placing her behind him as he drew his sword with a rasp of metal.

Figures emerged from the shelter of the trees — four or five men clad in rough unbleached tunics and long cloaks with hoods that hid their faces. All of them were armed with staves and knives, and one of them held a crossbow at the ready, pointing at Edgar's heart. Staring from behind the wolfskin cloak, Lynette saw a huge man stroll slowly into sight with a drawn sword.

"A pretty prize, lads," he said from the depths of his hood. "Forgive us, my lord," with a bow for Edgar; "but we poor folk must earn a living where we can. We don't kill — unless we're forced. Put up your sword, my lord, and there need be no bloodshed."

"Curse you!" Ralf cried, shaking his stick. "We're poor folk ourselves. Can't you see that?"

"Leave it, Ralf," Edgar said quietly. "We are outnumbered. Very well, my friend, what is it you want?"

"Your horses, for a start, my lord."

"Take them."

"And your sword?"

Edgar hesitated, his blade catching the light. Without it he would be unarmed save for his dagger. Shaking with terror, Lynette realised that he had little choice, not against a crossbow; then she saw the bowman raise his weapon, sighting along it at Edgar.

"No!" As the scream was torn from her, Edgar whirled and threw her to the ground. Her cloak flew up and covered her head so that she was blinded. She heard shouts and the sound of fighting, a horrible choking cry, and as she struggled for air Edgar bent beside her, hauling her to her feet. Without ceremony he dragged her to his horse, forced her onto it and himself leapt up behind her, an arm round her waist as he spurred the charger to a gallop.

Lynette caught a last glimpse of Ralf fighting valiantly with one of the brigands. It all happened so swiftly that she barely had time to breathe, let alone think. They raced through the woods, bending to avoid low branches, sometimes jumping over briars, dappled light and shade flying so fast that Lynette's head began to spin. Had it not been for the firm arm around her she would have fallen from the horse. She flopped helplessly, tossing with every movement of the charger, until merciful oblivion claimed her.

When she came round she found herself lying on something soft, with branches spreading above her, black against the red of the sunset. Nearby a murmur of voices sounded.

As she sat up, holding her aching head and wondering where she was, she saw a small group of men gathered by a fire in a clearing not far away — the band of robbers! Then a dark figure detached itself and came towards her holding a cup.

"You are safe now," Edgar of the Moor said, kneeling beside her. "Take some wine, my lady."

Furious, Lynette dashed the cup from his hands, spattering the contents all down his black tunic. "How dare you! This was a plot! I should have listened to Ralf. He said you were not to be trusted. You have abducted me!"

He considered her with cool derision in his eyes. "You might consider it abduction."

"I do! I do! You are everything they say you are — wicked and black-hearted. Sir Miles will kill you."

"I dare say he would try." Edgar

replied. "But you are in no danger, my lady."

"No danger? How can I be in no danger with those — those brigands as companions?"

"My lady," Edgar said softly, "they will not harm you. I promise you that not one of my men would lift a finger to harm my wife."

She stared at him in the gathering darkness, horrified. "Your wife?"

"Aye, my lady. I told them we were wed — for your protection, you understand. You had best play the part well, if you wish to remain safe."

3

THE dawn chorus woke Lynette. She was surprised to find that she had slept and was quite as warm and comfortable as she would have been at home, though her mouth tasted sour and her stomach rumbled. She remembered that she had refused food and drink the previous night, after which she had been left alone to sleep.

Around her the hastily-made camp was being struck, the ashes of the fire kicked about and covered with earth and twigs while the brigands lashed packs onto their horses, but when she sat up one of the men came over with a mug of wine and a hunk of dark rye bread. She was tempted to refuse again, but her stomach growled in protest and she took the refreshment.

"He said you would not starve

yourself," the man said with a grin that showed crooked teeth. "I'm Ned. I'm to look after you."

Swallowing thickly, Lynette glanced round at the activity. Edgar was nowhere in sight.

"He's gone," Ned told her. "Had something important to do. But he'll be back, never fear. He wouldn't desert you."

"Desert me?" Lynette spat. She was about to add that she was a prisoner and not Edgar's wife, but she recalled what might happen if these ruffians knew she had no husband to protect her. Since they were Edgar's men they would respect their leader's wife, so for the moment she would have to pretend.

"Where is my servant Ralf?" she asked. "If you have harmed him — "

Ned looked puzzled, scratching at his shaggy brown hair. "Your servant?"

"Yes! He was with us yesterday when you attacked us."

"Well, I don't know what became of

him," Ned said with a shrug. "Eat up, my lady. We must be on our way."

"To where?"

The grin broke out again on his face. "To where we're going. And I hope you'll behave yourself. I've orders to leave you free as long as you go quietly with us." He stood up and ambled away, leaving Lynette to consider her situation.

It was hopeless to think of escape, she knew. There were five outlaws and all were armed. Without even a friend to talk to, she must go with them.

As she finished her breakfast, she noticed the blanket which had kept her warm all night. It was no blanket, but the black cloak owned by Edgar of the Moor. The wolfskin fur had been against her face as she slept.

Shuddering, she stood up and threw off the cloak, wondering what Edgar had used for a cover, and what he was wearing now to keep him warm in the chilly morning air. But she thrust the thought aside angrily. What did she care for his comfort? He was neither prince nor wizard, but a common brigand. He had probably abducted her to secure a ransom from her father, or perhaps from Miles.

Ned returned to stand beside her, shifting awkwardly from foot to foot. He took the mug from her and thrust a brown bundle into her hands, scratching the back of his neck.

"Begging your pardon, my lady, but I was told to have you wear these. The tunic will go on top of your own clothes — if you hitch up your skirts. And the cloak is fairly clean."

Avoiding her look of outrage, he bent and swept up Edgar's cloak before departing.

Lynette looked at the garments in distaste. This was too much! Was she expected to dress like a peasant — and a male peasant at that? Oh, she looked forward to recounting these humilitations to Miles when she was set free. Miles would make Edgar of the Moor pay for his insults.

She pulled the wide tunic over her head. It hung below her knees but showed a wide hem of her own tunic, so she scooped up the back of her skirts and tucked them into her girdle at the front. Such swathing served in place of the loose under-drawers such as men wore and her own tunic was now hidden, though she looked lumpish. Pulling a face, she swirled the long cloak around her and stood defiantly, waiting for further instructions.

The party mounted up and to Lynette's surprise Ned brought her own grey mare from behind a bank of bushes.

"We rescued it," he explained.

"Rescued?" Lynette echoed. "You mean you captured it, too. No doubt you will sell it at the first settlement we come to."

To her astonishment, Ned laughed, shaking his head. "I always said it would be an unusual woman who captured Edgar of the Moor. Sell it, my lady? No, not unless you say so.

My lord would have my head first. Oh
— excuse me."

He leaned forward and drew the
wide hood of the cloak over her head
to hide her hair, winking at her as if
she were party to a conspiracy.

"Ned — " Lynette decided on a
gamble. "Did you know that your lord
abducted me? I was peacefully on my
way home when — "

"Oh, aye, I know all about that,"
he said cheerfully. "Don't you worry.
You're safe with us."

"But you don't seem to understand!"
she protested.

"Of course I do!" Ned laughed. "I
have enough trouble with my own wife.
Marriage is all the same, for nobles
or commoners. But Sir Edgar'll soon
settle you down. You should see him
train wild horses to the bridle. Now up
you get, my lady. We must be away."

Lynette obeyed almost without
thought, settling astride her mount
still seething with anger. Trained to
the bridle, indeed! Was that how Edgar

of the Moor regarded her — as a mettlesome filly ripe for the breaking?

They rode all day, keeping always to the woods and deserted places, skirting round settlements and pausing only to eat of the simple fare they carried in their packs. Ned kept a leading rein on Lynette's mare, so she could not have escaped even if she had known where to go. All she knew was that they were heading east, away from Braxby.

No-one except Ned spoke to her. The others seemed wary of her, though they conversed among themselves in that strange accent which, when muttered, was unintelligible to her. From Ned all she had were enquiries after her comfort and occasional remarks about. the countryside through which they passed.

They came to a broad, marshy area across which they rode in haste towards the deep forests in the distance. The horses splashed through a wide ford across the river Trent and once they came upon a group of peasants out cutting rushes, but the peasants ignored them and Lynette knew it would do her no good to call for help.

She was worried about Ralf, sorry she had not listened to his warnings about Edgar of the Moor, and most of all she grew more and more concerned for her father. When he heard she was missing he would be frantic, and already he was very sick, possibly dying. She vowed she would never forgive Edgar for any of this.

That night they camped in thick woodland, where they ate roasted rabbit, fresh-caught and cooked on sticks over the fire. When the guards were set for the night Ned brought her the wolfskin cloak, but she pushed it aside and huddled in the thin mantle he had given her earlier. The April night grew cold, however, and after shivering for a while she drew Edgar's cloak round her, luxuriating in its warmth even while she planned vengeance on its owner.

She dreamed that she told Miles

of what had occurred. She saw him riding out in golden armour to avenge her while she waited in a high room of a castle keep and saw him returning victorious. In her dream she ran soundlessly down a circling stair, coming into a courtyard. And there was Miles, smiling at her, with Edgar's blood on his hands.

She woke suddenly, a cry of horror on her lips, and lay trembling in the first light of dawn. Wildly she wondered why her feelings were so at war with her common sense. She hated Edgar for what he had done to her, but she could not deny that part of her wished he would come and look at her with laughter in his eyes.

Around her, Edgar's men began to stir for yet another day in the saddle. Stiff and sore, now totally bewildered, Lynette ate her simple breakfast and hauled herself back onto her horse, resigning herself to her fate. There seemed to be no other course.

The country grew wilder, hillier, and

often they took wide detours to avoid an inhabited valley. Because they moved most of the time through trees there was seldom anything to see but oak woods, grass and bushes.

Lynette caught the gist of conversation among the band. They were discussing whether to stop for dinner. Some complained of weariness and hunger, but others argued that it was best to go on, to reach 'Wolf Rock', wherever that might be.

"We'll go on," Ned's voice rang out eventually. "It should be less than an hour. Then you can rest."

To Lynette's surprise, the argument ceased apart from a little grumbling and a few sidelong looks at their captive. She glanced at Ned, puzzled by him. Was he their leader? It had certainly not been Ned who led the initial ambush, for that man had been a huge, burly fellow, one whom she did not recall seeing since. Perhaps Ralf had injured him in the scuffle.

Dear, brave Ralf! Where was he?

Had he found his way home with his tale of treachery, or was he — dreadful thought — still lying in the greenwood?

"There it is!" Ned sang out, pointing to a hill ahead. Trees cloaked its slopes and the valley in between, but a big rock stood out to one side, a pale shape like the slavering jaws of a wolf with laid back ears.

Quickening their pace, the party rode down through the wooded valley and up the further side, pausing in the shade of the great rock. Lynette's muscles would hardly work as she slid from the saddle and painfully stretched her aching body.

While they dined on bread and cheese, with a little rabbit meat left from the previous night, the youngest member of the band — a lad named Ulf — scrambled to the top of the rock and peered back in the direction from whence they had come, as if looking for something.

"Day after tomorrow, we shall be there," Ned said, seating himself beside

Lynette. "You'll like the valley, my lady, though you'll have to watch out for Mistress Johanna. She's always thought Sir Edgar was her property. She won't be pleased he's got wed without a word to her."

"Mistress Johanna?" Lynette repeated, already disliking the woman. "Who is she?"

"She's the widow of Sir Edgar's uncle. He brought her to the valley after her husband died. Ever since then she's been acting like she's the mistress."

As Lynette pondered this information, one of the men called to Ned to join them and the little band began to argue in low voices, with many a suspicious glance thrown at Lynette. She saw that Ned was defending her, though she could not make out what any of them were saying.

Then a low whistle came from Ulf perched high on the rock. He called, "Someone coming."

"Can you see who it is?" Ned asked.

"Not yet," came the reply.

Fear caught at Lynette's heart, but it was followed almost immediately by hope. Perhaps they had been followed. Perhaps the newcomer was Miles, hurrying to rescue her.

A few minutes later, however, such hopes died when Ulf called excitedly, "Yes, it's him. It's Sir Edgar."

"Good," said Ned, adding to the rest of his band, "Now you be content. I'll tell him what you said."

He hurried off on foot and was soon out of sight among the trees in the valley.

Aware of the ill-feeling towards her, Lynette scrambled up and stood with her back against the rock, her hands clenched round folds of the rough cloak, while the three brigands stood a little apart throwing dark looks at her and muttering among themselves.

Young Ulf slid from the rock to land lightly beside her, flashing his bright smile. "You'll feel better now, my lady."

"Yes," Lynette said, though her feelings were in question. She was relieved that Edgar was near, but only because he could still the restless murmurings of his men. She still feared the news he might bring.

Among the trees below she saw him leading his horse as he walked deep in discussion with Ned. Slowly they came up the hill. The black charger's flanks gleamed with sweat and it breathed in snorts, as if it had been ridden hard, while Edgar himself was travel-stained and looked weary. Lynette straightened herself defiantly as his eyes met hers and swept over her, then to her fury those eyes lit up with grim humour at the sight she presented.

He bowed low, so low she knew he was mocking her. "My lady, you make a most convincing brigand."

"I was not given much choice!" Lynette retorted. "Pray, what is to be my fate? Must I continue to be humiliated?"

Ned chuckled to himself, saying,

"Your lady has a fine spirit, my lord."

"Aye, I know," Edgar said ruefully.

"Will you answer me?" Lynette cried, quivering with anger. "How much longer am I to be treated in this way? Until my father pays — "

The words choked off as Edgar stepped forward, caught her in his arms and kissed her, his mouth hard and unyielding on hers. For a moment Lynette fought, her small fists puny weapons against his strength, but slowly her struggles ceased. She had never before been kissed, never guessed that it could cause her head to spin and her heart to thud. Near fainting, she leaned weakly on Edgar, feeling his arms like iron bands around her.

"I told her you'd soon tame her, my lord," Ned laughed as Lynette hid her burning face against Edgar's shoulder. She was ashamed now that she had given in so feebly.

"Leave her to me," Edgar said. "The rest of you can go home now. There's no sign of pursuit. We'll follow you shortly, but first I must rest."

Wrenching away from him, Lynette threw herself to the ground, huddled into a ball of misery. What did he intend to do with her when they were alone? She wished now that the others would stay.

A short while later the band rode away, more cheerful now that they were leaving Lynette behind. Edgar rubbed his horse down and set it to graze before sitting a few feet from Lynette. He began to eat as if he were starving, while Lynette watched him from her eye corner wondering where he had been.

When he had finished his meal, Edgar drank deep from a wine skin and turned his eyes towards Lynette. "I have hardly eaten or slept since we parted. Will you forgive me if I rest?"

"You may do as you please — my lord," she replied bitterly. "Why ask my permission? I am your captive, after all."

"Indeed you are." Edgar said, and

stretched himself out on his wolfskin cloak, pulling its corner round him. In a very short time Lynette could tell from his breathing that he was asleep.

She looked around her, considering courses of action. The sun stood midway down the sky to her right, shining through the branches of the trees. Her own horse was still tethered to a bush, fed and rested, while Edgar's black charger twitched as it grazed. The animal was almost worn out.

Not far from where she sat, Edgar slept on his side. He had unbuckled his sword and placed it beneath him, out of her sight, but in his belt a dagger with a jewelled hilt rested in a sheath. She could see the gleam of the jewels under the shadow of his cloak.

Very slowly, being careful not to make a sound, Lynette crept towards him, pausing to look at his face. Even in sleep he still looked weary, lines drawn in his tanned face and dark circles beneath his eyes. His hair ruffled softly in the wind, making him seem younger. Lynette watched him for a moment, disturbed by the tender feelings which warred with her anger.

Then, shaking herself, she put out a hand to the hilt of his dagger and gently tried to ease it free. It was fastened with a thong! She cried out as Edgar's elbow clamped down on her hand and he sat up, black eyes ablaze in his craggy face.

"Do you hate me so much?" he demanded. "To kill me while I sleep?"

"No!" Lynette cried. "I wanted the dagger for my protection. I was going to take my horse and — Sir, you are hurting me!"

He released her instantly and she sat back on her heels, rubbing her aching hand while her eyes filled with tears.

"I did not intend to harm you," she said. "I swear I did not."

Edgar rubbed his face tiredly, shaking his head. "None would have blamed you. But to escape from me would only put you in greater danger. You would lose yourself in these hills. There are bands of brigands wandering, and still a few wolves. Suppose your horse stepped in a rabbit hole and you were stranded, alone?"

Her eyes grew wide in her pale face. "I had not thought. I wanted only to escape. Oh, why have you brought me here? Where have you been? Did you see my father?"

"No, I did not. Do not ask me where I have been, my lady. As to why I brought you, why — " he shrugged " — I had my reasons. Now forgive me, but I must sleep. Keep watch for me. Wake me if you hear anything. But do not stray. For your own safety."

"You treat me like a child," Lynette said as he lay down again, but he made no reply.

Knowing that he was right about the dangers lurking in the wooded hills, she sat with her back against the rock, listening for any unusual sound. Somewhere nearby a stream trickled. She heard the snorting of the horses, the cries of small animals and the songs of birds; then she must have slept, for she came awake with a jerk to find the sun gone behind the hill, filling the valley with shadow while the sky flamed with banners of gold.

She strained her ears to listen as she rose and peered through the trees in all directions, but the woods remained still. Sighing to herself, Lynette walked to where her mare waited patiently. She stroked the soft nose and thought about Braxby, wondering how her father fared, and where was Ralf?

"My lady!" Edgar said sharply from behind her. "Ah — there you are. It's time we were leaving. I have slept longer than I intended."

"You were very tired," Lynette said, watching as he stretched himself.

"Aye, that I was."

"Do you — do you know what became of Ralf, sir? I am much concerned for him. He has been my friend since we were children. And my father — I told you he was sick. He will be worried about me."

Edgar strolled to her side and looked down at her gravely. "Ralf is safe and well. That much I know. Apart from a lump on the head, he was unharmed. He fought bravely for you."

"Yes, he would," Lynette said, her chin lifting defiantly. "Even against a band of ruffians better armed than he. And what have you done with him, sir? Tossed him in a dungeon?"

"Would you believe me if I said I had sent him home with a message for your father?"

"As I suspected!" she exclaimed. "You sent him to demand a ransom. But my father has no money. He cannot pay. Unless — you expect him to apply to Miles for help, do you? It is Miles who will have to pay for my release."

"Oh, he will pay," Edgar said grimly, his eyes narrowed. "Indeed he will pay. I shall make sure of that."

She was appalled by the menace in his voice and drew back from him, staring up at his taut face. "Is that how a true knight settles his quarrels?" she asked, her voice hoarse. "Through helpless women? You abducted me because I am betrothed to Miles of Louth. That was your only reason — that you hate Miles!"

"And tonight," Edgar said, his glance flicking her up and down, "I shall give him reason to hate me more. Take off that cloak and tunic. Since we are safe from pursuit there is no need for you to look like a peasant any longer."

Lynette hesitated; feeling that the unfeminine clothes were perhaps a protection against him. What did he intend to do when night fell? What could make Miles hate him more?

"Take them off," Edgar said, his lips twisting as if he read her thoughts. He reached for the saddle of his own horse and tossed her the cloak which lay there — her own cloak, with its lining of sheepskin shorn from Braxby lambs.

Moving a distance away from him, Lynette threw off the cloak which

Ned had given her and undid her rope belt. The coarse tunic pulled off over her head and she let her skirts loose from her girdle, shaking out their crumpled folds.

"That's better," Edgar said.

Flushing under his gaze, Lynette swirled her own cloak about her, holding it so that it covered her completely. She tilted her chin to stare at her captor.

"Where are we bound?" she asked.

"Why, to our wedding, my lady," Edgar replied with a bow. "Come, let us be on our way. We have several miles to cover before nightfall, and the priest is waiting."

His figure seemed to blur before her eyes and she swayed momentarily, swallowing hard to clear the lump from her throat. "The priest? Wedding? If you expect me to marry you after — "

"You had best marry me," he said softly. "My men were beginning to suspect. Why do you think I stopped you from speaking of a ransom in front of them? They do not like the trouble I may be bringing by taking you to the valley, but if you are my wife they will accept it."

"You — " Lynette managed, licking suddenly-dry lips. "You would force me to wed you?"

"I give you a choice. Be my wife, or face the wrath of my people. They have not much love for Normans, my lady. I am your only hope of protection."

"And if I refuse?" she breathed.

"There is a third choice — stay here and face the night and the wolves. It may be a more pleasant fate than you will face should my people find out for sure that we are not wed. Now come!" He sounded impatient. "Am I so ill-favoured that you will refuse to take me for husband even at the risk of your life? I am not a poor man. Nor am I harsh, unless provoked. You could do worse."

"But I am betrothed to Sir Miles!" Lynette protested.

"I am not like to forget it. But a

betrothal is not final until the marriage vows have been spoken. A betrothal can be broken. Suppose I tell you that Sir Miles has already broken it?"

"Then I would not believe you! You would tell any lies to confuse me. I know Miles. He is the king's champion. Faithful. Honourable. Unlike you, sir. Were it not for his faithfulness to his duty I would be his wife now and beyond your evil designs."

"Enough!" Edgar cried, and strode across the grass to toss her up into his arms. He all but threw her into the saddle and swiftly mounted his own horse, leading the way through the dusk-filled woods.

He cannot force me! Lynette thought wildly. But the alternatives were frightening — facing the woods alone in the dark, or risking the anger of Edgar's men, who had already been muttering against her.

She must wed him for her own safety. But she would deny him his husbandly rights. One day she would be free and then she would have the marriage declared void, because she had been under duress. She would come to Miles unsullied, in the end.

Ahead of her, Edgar was a solid shadow in the fathering twilight, leading her horse by a rein. She directed thoughts of hatred at his broad back, vowing not to let him touch her, but even as the thought came she remembered the feelings which had flooded through her when he kissed her, and the tenderness she had experienced as he lay sleeping. She wondered how long her heart could withstand a siege of that kind.

From somewhere far away there came the mournful howling of a wolf. Lynette had never heard such a sound, though she had listened to travellers' tales, and now she experienced the prickle along her spine as the eerie sound floated beneath the first twinkling star.

Edgar dropped back a few paces, saying over his shoulder, "They are far away. Do not be afraid."

"I am not afraid," she replied haughtily, and realised it was the truth. With Edgar by her side she had no fear of wolves; her only fears were of Edgar himself, his strength and the strange effect he had on her.

Overhead the sky darkened as if ink were being poured into a pool. Lynette wondered how Edgar could see his way, but he kept going, twisting a path among the trees, up hill and down.

Just before the last light died from the sky, Lynette glimpsed a flickering up ahead, a yellow glow that came and went behind the boles of the trees. She realised that it was a fire, built inside a cave.

At the edge of the small clearing Edgar dismounted and walked forward alone until he was outlined against the firelight in the low cave mouth.

"Machel!" he called softly. "Machel, it is Edgar of the Moor."

"Ho, Edgar!" The voice came from somewhere in the woods and a man stepped into sight. He was dressed in a long robe with the hood slung back to reveal thick grey hair and a beard forked after the old Saxon fashion. By his side padded a big grey dog.

The man embraced Edgar warmly, welcoming him as an old friend, and Edgar bent to pet the dog.

Lynette looked again, catching her breath. The animal was like no dog she had ever seen — big, shaggy, grey, its fur was like the lining of Edgar's cloak. A wolf! Yet it seemed tame and allowed Edgar to stroke its great head.

The two men spoke quietly together for a few minutes, too low for Lynette to hear what was said.

Then Edgar strode back to her and lifted her from the saddle to the ground.

"Have you made your choice?" he asked in an undertone.

"I have," she replied, "though little enough choice it is. I warn you, sir, you will not find me a willing bride."

"But you will go through with the marriage?"

"I will, since I must. But — here?"

"Here," Edgar agreed. "Machel is an ordained priest, even though he chooses to live as a hermit. We shall be truly wed, before God and under the law of the land. That I promise you."

Lynette smiled bleakly to herself. "Is that meant to comfort me? Very well. Since my lord is a barbarian, let us wed in barbarian style."

His hand closed round hers, as if to make sure she did not run away, and he led her towards the cave. Had the slightest chance of escape presented itself, Lynette would have taken it. She gazed nervously round at the red-lit walls rough-hewn by nature, and at the wolf which now lay silent, firelight gleaming in its half-closed eyes.

"Do not fear Lupus," Edgar said. "Machel has raised him from a cub."

"Did he raise you, too?" Lynette could not resist the jibe. "In the woods, among wolves?"

He looked down at her, his eyes veiled though she fancied she saw them gleam. "You will soon find out whether you have married a wild man, my lady."

The priest Machel waited at the back of the cave, a golden crucifix on a long chain hanging round his neck and in his hands a goblet. On the wall behind him another cross, beautifully carved of oak, gave the place the semblance of a church.

While the old hermit spoke the words in sonorous Latin, Lynette stared at the cross behind him. She thought about Miles, renewing her vow to keep herself for her true betrothed, and she said silent prayers for her father's health.

A few minutes later she found herself standing beside Edgar, her hand in his, as if she were having some strange dream. She turned to look up at him, bemused, and he bent to kiss her cheek.

"The only ring I have to give you,"

he said, tugging at his little finger, is this one.

The ring was gold with a stone made of black jet. It fitted only on her index finger, and when it was placed there she stared down at it, thinking that she must soon wake up in her own bed at Braxby. Surely the past few days had been nothing but a nightmare.

"Care for her well, Edgar," the old man said. "And you, my lady — " he took her face between cool hands that felt like parchment " — you have found yourself a good man. Be a good wife to him in return."

Lynette stared into eyes of a clear grey — honest, trustworthy eyes, she thought. But the old man knew very little about the real Edgar. Did he guess that the 'good man' was a leader of brigands, an abductor of women, and probably other things far worse?

She made no attempt to speak her thoughts aloud. They seemed out of place at that time as Machel kissed her brow benevolently and wished her well. She could hardly believe it, but her senses told her she had become the lawful wedded wife of Edgar of the Moor, the black Saxon.

4

THE sun woke Lynette as it slanted through the trees straight into her eyes. She was alone at the back of the cave, lying on a bed of branches, and the places where the two men had slept, either side of the fire, had been cleared. Now the fire smoked fitfully beneath a pile of ashes.

Lynette lay for a moment recalling the fire glowing bright in the cave while she and Edgar, with Machel, sat on boulders and ate a delicious stew which the old man had prepared. She had fallen asleep to the sound of their voices chatting softly about old times and old friends, and for some reason she had been annoyed that Edgar could ignore her on their wedding night. Not that she wished him to pay her attention. Had he done so she would have fought him. But she was piqued that he had not even given her an opportunity to show him her scorn.

She sat up, twisting the ring on her first finger. It felt strange and heavy, the sun gleaming off the facets of the jet stone.

"So you are awake," Edgar said, ducking into the cave with an armful of brushwood which he dumped behind a boulder. He had brushed down his black tunic and his dark hair was wet at the edges from washing. "I thought you would sleep the day through."

"I am not used to riding so many miles," Lynette replied irritably. She stood up, pulling a face as she shook out her tunic. It was crumpled and stained and her hair needed a comb and fresh braiding. Humiliation piled on humiliation and she felt very ill-tempered.

"There is a stream not far away," Edgar said. "But I fear clean clothes must wait until we reach the valley. As to riding — if you wish, you may ride with me."

Lynette flushed, thinking of a day spent so close to him that their bodies must constantly touch. "I shall ride my mare, thank you," she said coolly.

"You did not scorn to ride behind your serving man," he reminded her.

"Ralf is my friend!"

Edgar regarded her across the cave, his dark eyes expressionless. "And I," he said softly, "am your husband."

"How could I forget it?" Lynette flared. "What woman could be insensible to the gentle ways of your courting, the magnificence of the wedding ceremony and the honour you accord me? In truth, my head is quite turned by the romance of it all. And as you honour your bride, so shall I honour my husband!"

"You think Miles of Louth would have done better?" he asked.

She clenched her hands, shaking with anger. "Do not even speak his name! You are not fit to breathe the same air as he."

"I see that a night's rest has not

improved your temper," Edgar said levelly. "My lady, I weary of your termagent tongue. If you wish to refresh yourself I will show you the stream. But please let us have done with these tantrums. You only sully a beautiful morning."

Speechless with rage, she followed him from the cave and found herself in a deep wooded valley. Edgar led her through the trees to where a clear stream danced over a rocky bed, coming from somewhere on the hillside above.

"Can you find your way back to the cave?" he asked. "I will go and prepare breakfast. But do not be long. And, my lady, do not be so foolish as to run away."

Lynette contented herself with giving him a look charged with hatred; then she bent by the stream and splashed its chilly water on her face and hands. She would have liked to bathe, but the water was cold, she had no towel, and with Edgar near at hand she baulked at the thought of removing her clothes.

Sooner or later, she knew, he would attempt to make her his wife in every way, and she had no intention of tempting him to make it sooner.

Her toilette completed, she lifted her skirts free of the grass and trailed back down the valley to the cave. Strangely, the clear air of the morning had the effect of raising her spirits. She was in no immediate danger and the sun shone brightly as it lifted above the hills, making the birds sing joyfully as they enticed their mates to help build nests.

She was reminded suddenly of a ballad she had heard sung by a minstrel: a wonderful song about a great lord who fell in love with a lady on her way to be married. One look at her was enough to send him swooping down to carry her off to his castle, where they lived happily for the rest of their days. Perhaps that was the way of it with Edgar — perhaps he had been struck by her beauty and could not bear the thought of her becoming the wife of his rival.

The idea made her laugh to herself as she came within sight of the cave mouth, where Edgar sat on a rock sharpening his dagger with a stone. He looked up, his own face lightening as he saw her smile.

"Mountain water must have magic in it," he said.

"Perhaps it does," Lynette replied, but she had no intention of letting him think the battle was won. "I saw my reflection. I was reminded of the compliments Sir Miles showered on me, and I began to think of what he will do to you when he captures you. It improved my spirits."

"Are you so sure of him?" Edgar asked, a shadow darkening his eyes.

"Sure as I am that the sun will rise each day. Miles is as constant as the sun, and as fair. His memory will go with me everywhere — whatever indignities you try to inflict on me."

Dropping the dagger to the ground, Edgar sprang to his feet and grasped her wrist, his other arm drawing her hard against him. His eyes glowed in his dark face as he stared down at her, his gaze flicking over her features and finally resting on her mouth.

Lynette's skin broke into a million tiny prickles and her green eyes grew wide, like a hunted fawn. She was mesmerised by his nearness, unable to struggle.

"Sir — "

The gasp was cut off as he dropped his mouth to hers, one hand caught behind her head while the other pressed her close to his body. Her senses swooped and she fought an urge to wrap her arms about him and return his embrace, though the urge grew stronger, becoming a need. As she was about to give in to it he released her, his breath coming hoarse and uneven and his eyes alight with desire.

"Are you thinking of Sir Miles now?" he asked harshly.

Her head was still spinning and she feared her legs would buckle under her, but she found strength from somewhere and spat, "Yes! I shall always be thinking of him. Every time you touch me, I shall think of Miles. You are my husband and may do with me as you please, but though you take my body you can never force my heart to belong to you. That is for Miles, for the king's own true champion."

With a muttered curse, Edgar swung away and picked up his dagger. "Then live with your childish dreams, my lady. I shall not inflict myself upon you more. Come, eat. It is past time we were away."

As they breakfasted in the cave, several yards apart, Lynette watched her wedded lord, who did not look at her once. Was it possible that he was jealous? Could it be that this Saxon brigand cared for her?

"Where is Machel?" she asked when the silence grew too much to bear.

"Gone into the hills. He comes to the cave only at night. He does not enjoy the company of human beings.

And," he added bitterly, "there are times when I agree with him."

"Have you known him for a long time?"

"For most of my life." He glanced at her briefly, his eyes bleak. "My father was a wolf, did you not know? I was raised in the forest and learned the ways of magic. I practise my spells on Prince Henry, to my own evil ends, and everyone hates me."

"If that were true," Lynette replied, "why did you not cast a spell on me and make me the willing bride you wish me to be?"

"Maybe I shall do so," he said, "when I have the time."

She rose from her boulder, brushing crumbs from her tunic. "If that is meant to frighten me, sir, it misses its mark. I do not believe you have magic powers, whatever people say. As to being fathered by a wolf — you show little evidence of that in your looks, though your behaviour is savage. I think it is a tale, you are pleased to encourage, to add mystery."

For a moment Edgar kept his head bent so that she could not see his face, then he stood up and looked at her with a wry smile twisting one corner of his hard mouth. "And what is the truth, in your opinion?"

"The truth, sir? Why, that you are a mere brigand — a man who walks outside the law. Prince Henry's patronage gives you a semblance of respectability, but you are more at home living wild, among your band of outlaws. Like all dangerous animals, you will be hunted, and captured, eventually."

To her surprise, Edgar laughed. "You have courage, my lady. I intend to take you to my lair and keep you there. I shall make you as wild as I am. Does the thought not disquiet you? Will Sir Miles still wish to take as his bride a lady who has consorted with brigands?"

"Nothing you can do will change me," Lynette said, tossing her head. "You forget that I am protected by the memory of my own true knight."

Edgar only stroked his chin, narrowed eyes gleaming.

"You asked me," he said, "why I did not cast a spell on you. The answer is, my lady, that I am not at all interested in making you a 'willing bride'. I have married you for your own protection, nothing more."

He ducked out of the cave and strolled to where the horses were tethered, leaving Lynette feeling as though he had slapped her.

All day they travelled, alternately riding and walking, through country that grew wilder with every mile. They were slowly climbing up towards bleak hills which Lynette glimpsed looming ahead, and when she looked back, at every crest they reached, all that lay behind was a great sea of trees. No longer did they take detours round habitations, for there were no habitations. They had reached the Pennines and turned north.

As her strength ebbed, so depression

sat on her more heavily. They had come so far that she began to doubt if she would ever see her father or her home again, and how could Miles possibly find her in this wilderness of forests and hills?

During the afternoon, clouds billowed up from the west, obscuring the sun and turning the air cold.

"We shall have rain by nightfall," Edgar remarked as they walked side by side leading the horses.

Lynette had been thinking the same. She said sourly, "Does your magic foretell it?"

"Are you tired?" he enquired, looking at her in concern. "I hope to find shelter before long. Just a little further."

"Your interest in my well-being is touching, if a little tardy,". she returned. "But since I am the wife of a brigand I must train myself to the saddle, I suppose."

"Only for two more days."

Lynette bent her head, biting back tears of weariness. Two more days seemed an endless time. "And then?"

"Then you may rest and recover your strength."

"Ah, yes. At your headquarters camp, I assume? Where a woman named Johanna impatiently awaits your coming."

"Johanna?" Edgar said sharply. "Who told you of her?"

"Your man Ned mentioned her. I trust I shall not be expected to fight with teeth and nails over you. That is how matters of the heart are settled in the forest, is it not?" She sighed heavily, rubbing a hand across her face. "My heart would not be in it, I fear. Johanna may have you, for aught I care."

"She cannot have me," Edgar said. "You are my wedded wife, for good or ill. And Johanna will accept you as such. It was foolish of Ned to speak of such matters. What else did he tell you?"

Lynette looked up at the lowering clouds, feeling the first drops of rain on her face. "That the sky is blue, that here was a hare and there the track of a fox. He prattled about nothing, to say it clearly — though he did say that you would train me to the bridle, as you train wild horses. Perhaps he spoke wisely there, for even the strongest horse would be docile after being dragged through the endless forest for days."

"The necessity for such a journey distresses me," Edgar said. "I did not subject you to it from any choice of mine."

Astonished, Lynette looked up at him. "Then whose choice was it, pray? Not mine, for sure."

"It was for your safety."

"Indeed! You continue to spin me a thread of lies, sir. I know what your object was — to take me so far from country that was familiar to me that I would have no hope of escape or rescue. Do you think me a simple peasant to believe it is for my protection?"

Edgar's face was unreadable, blank as a stone wall. "There were those who wished you harm."

"I know there were! You, for one, and your band of uncouth thieves! They attacked us, to divert poor Ralf's attention while you carried me off. Your excuses cannot make me forget the evidence of my own senses."

He stopped walking and said abruptly, "We will ride. We must reach shelter before the storm comes."

Bending to link his hands for her foot, he helped her into the saddle. Her muscles ached in protest and she gazed disgustedly down at Edgar's hard brown face.

"My lady," he said quietly, a hand on her wrist. "I understand your confusion, but one day you will thank me."

A weary laugh escaped her. "If ever that day comes, sir, then I shall know that you are a wizard indeed. Nothing would induce me to forgive you for what has passed, let alone to thank you."

"As you will," Edgar said, and turned to his own black charger.

The rain began to drip steadily from the grey sky, obliging Lynette to put up the hood of her cloak. She rode with her eyes on the ground, letting Edgar lead where he would.

At length, at a place no different from the rest, Edgar stopped and glanced at the sky as if to judge the height of the invisible sun.

"We shall not reach the place before nightfall," he said. "I misjudged our pace, and it was well after dawn when we set out. We must stay here."

"Here?" Disconsolately, Lynette peered from her hood at the crowding trees and bushes.

"An outlaw's wife must often sleep under the stars," Edgar told her.

"I would not object if I thought there would be stars," Lynette replied. "But as it is raining — Oh, very well. I may as well die of a fever as of shame." She was so tired that it no longer seemed to matter what happened. All she wanted to do was to lie down and sleep.

She sat wearily under a tree, drawing the hooded cloak around her, watching in wonderment as Edgar set about hacking branches from the trees. In a short time he had erected the skeleton of a bower and Lynette got up to help as she realised his plan.

Together they made a rounded tent of branches woven with trailing briars, and when it was done Edgar threw over it a blanket from the pack he carried behind his saddle, fastening it with grasses. Finally he brought the rough peasant cloak which Lynette had worn as a disguise and spread it on the floor of the bower before inviting her in out of the rain.

She hesitated, unwilling to share the small space with him, even if he was her husband.

"We must do without a fire," Edgar said. "Come in and shelter, my lady. Here's bread — somewhat stale, I fear. Cheese and herbs, and a skin of goat's milk given to us by Machel. I would snare you a hare, but I doubt you would eat it raw."

The sight of the food spread on the coarse cloak reminded Lynette that she had not eaten a proper meal in days. She crawled in through the small opening and, keeping as far from Edgar as she could, accepted her share of the food.

She ate slowly, partly to savour each mouthful and partly to delay the time they must lie down to sleep. The previous night she had had old Machel's presence to shield her, but tonight she was alone with Edgar and since she had been foolhardy enough to go through a ceremony of marriage with him she must expect him to demand his husbandly rights.

Glancing at him in the growing twilight, she wondered how long she could hold out against his greater strength. The memory of his arms around her made her skin quiver and when he looked up, sensing her eyes on him, she was obliged to turn away for fear he would read the conflict of her emotions.

"Is it so disagreeable, being wed to a brigand?" he asked softly. "You are fed, sheltered, and protected. What more can a woman wish for?"

"No doubt a Saxon woman would be content," Lynette managed through a throat that was suddenly constricted. "But I am a Norman. I have been taught, to expect more — comfort, consideration, and — "

"And?" Edgar prompted.

She flung back her head to glare at him. "And things that a barbarian like you would not understand!"

"You forget I am a knight of the realm," he said. "I have seen the ways of the court. Is it pretty speeches you want? Shall I say that you are beautiful — that your hair is the golden-red of a flaming sunset and your eyes like pools that reflect the summer woods?"

"Words! They come easy to you, sir."

"Aye, they trip off the tongue without

need for thought. But that is the game they play at court. I have become as adept a player as any man, though the game is not to my liking. A woman surely knows whether she is beautiful or not. She must see it in men's eyes."

"Even so," Lynette was piqued into objecting, "it is pleasant to hear compliments — if they are sincere."

"As Sir Miles's words were sincere?" Edgar enquired.

Inside the bower there was not enough light for her to see him clearly, but the mention of Miles brought back the hopelessness of her situation.

"Yes!" she cried. "He knelt before me and the truth shone from his face. With him it is not a game, nor would he use flattery to mock a lady. You are a disgrace to the rank of knight, sir!"

She cowered away as Edgar made a move in the darkness.

"Have no fear, my lady," he said derisively. "I intend also to disgrace the name of barbarian — I leave you the privacy of your bower. Sleep well."

Disconcerted, Lynette sat and watched him scramble from the bower into the rain that pattered heavily through the dusk. She heard him brush through the grass, then all was silence but for the rain.

She was relieved and yet she was torn by strange feelings of disappointment. Edgar never behaved as she expected him to behave, though of course she had no wish to have him bed with her. Of course she had not.

She lay down, angrily wrapping her cloak round her and turning her mind to memories of Miles kneeling in the candlelight, saying — what was it he had said? After Edgar's cynical dismissal of 'games they play at court', Miles's declarations of love rang false, like a cracked bell. How easily the words had come to his lips when he had been away for six long years. She must have been as much a stranger to him as he to her, yet he had instantly declared that she was the lady of his heart.

No, no! She must not think ill of Miles. Miles the true, Miles the valiant, Miles the king's champion with eyes like summer skies. But her traitor mind recalled the sweet words that Edgar had spoken, and though she knew he had been sporting with her the compliments tasted like wine when compared with the trite flattery she had heard from Miles. Was there no one to be trusted?

How she wished she could speak to her father and ask his advice, for she was beginning to realise how little she knew of life and of men. Sheltered at Braxby she had craved experience of the world, but after only a week she now longed for the safety of home. A picture of her father as she had left him came strongly to her. He had been so ill, so weak, begging her to seek Miles's protection. Dear heaven, would she ever see him again? Was he dead, even now, not knowing what had become of her?

In the blackness of night she wept

bitterly, hearing the constant rain pitter-pat on the roof of her bower until she thought the sound would make her run mad. She flung off her cloak and crawled to the opening of the shelter.

"Edgar! Edgar!"

Suppose he had left her. Suppose he had ridden off through the darkness and left her alone!

"Edgar!" The cry choked off as she sensed him approach, heard a stick snap beneath his feet and then his wet hand found hers.

"My lady?" he said softly.

With a shudder, the panic left her. She gulped down her tears and muttered, "You will be soaked to the skin. Come inside."

"Were you afraid?" he asked, touching her arms, then her face. "Are you weeping?"

"I — I was thinking of my father," Lynette said weakly. "I fear for him. And the night is so dark — and the rain — "

She felt the heavy wetness of his

cloak as he drew her down to lie beside him, though the wolf-fur-lining was dry and wonderfully warm. He laid it across her and pulled her to rest on his shoulder as if she were a child who needed comforting.

"Sleep," he murmured in her ear. "I will bring news of your father. Sleep, my lady. Do not fear the night, or the rain. My cloak is magic, did you know? It will protect us."

Knowing only that his presence had driven away the fears, Lynette laid her arm across him, comforted by his warmth and the muscular hardness of his body; then she drifted into dreams.

When she woke, Edgar had gone. Grey dawn light showed pale through the opening of the bower and somewhere nearby an animal cried as it hunted. Remembering what had happened, Lynette sat up, drawing her cloak close about her. She had panicked, that was all, and he had been kind. He might well show a little kindness when he was the cause of all her discomfort, both of body and mind.

Hearing him speaking to his horse nearby, she stiffened as she wondered what change in their relationship might have developed after the night's closeness. Part of her hoped that the tenderness would continue, but the rest of her was afraid.

"There is a mist this morning," Edgar said as he entered the bower, bringing her water to wash her hands. "Be swift, my lady. We have many miles to travel if we are to reach the valley tomorrow."

The bread was hard, but soaked in goat's milk it was palatable enough. While they ate, Edgar kept his distance, hardly looking at her and not speaking. His manner had become impersonal, maddening her.

While they rode through mists which slowly parted as the sun came up, they spoke only of things of the moment. Lynette wondered if he was aware, as she was, of the lightning force that sparked between them when their thighs touched as they rode side by side. Sometimes she fancied she caught a glimpse of that same lightning in his eyes, but in all other ways he remained aloof. Perhaps he did not sense the building awareness that made her blood beat faster and caused all her nerves to twitch every time he touched her.

They rode hard that day and as the sun went down they came to another cave. Edgar seemed pleased as he made a fire and gathered bracken for their beds, then he went off into the forest to hunt their supper.

He came back whistling, bringing a rabbit and a hare which he skinned with the skill of long practice and set them to roast on sticks above the fire. As the juices sizzled in the flames, Lynette's stomach worked. She had never been so hungry in her life before.

When Edgar broke off a piece of meat, offering it to her on the point of his dagger, she grabbed it and sank her teeth into the tasty flesh, pausing as she saw the amusement in his dark eyes.

"You will make a fine brigand's wife," he said. "And if you misbehave I shall know how to deal with you — I shall keep you short of food."

Annoyed, Lynette swallowed the morsel and retorted, "I would sooner starve than be an obedient wife to you. You will find you have made a bad bargain, sir."

"I already suspected it," Edgar said calmly. "But I hoped a Norman lady would not be so ill-bred as to accept her husband's protection and offer nothing in return. You are warmed by a fire I built. You eat the food I caught and cooked for you. And you will sleep on a bed I prepared with my own hands. What will you give me in return?"

Lynette stared at him, hoping he could not see that she was trembling. "My gratitude, sir."

"And if it is not enough?"

Leaping up, she backed away against the cave wall, glancing about her for something to use as a weapon. "Since I was wedded by force, I shall only be bedded by force. You will not easily overcome me, sir. I belong to Miles of Louth and will fight for what is his."

The firelight threw dancing reflections in his eyes, making him look like a demon. "It seems hardly worth the trouble," he said carelessly.

Her body felt on fire and her heart pounded uncomfortably. Not worth the trouble? How dare he! Was he made of stone?

"You are toying with me!" she cried.

"I mean what I say, my lady. Truly you are difficult to please. Make up your mind what it is to be wife or maid. It is all the same to me."

Infuriated by his indifference, Lynette said through her teeth, "I wish to be a wife — the wife of Sir Miles of Louth!"

"Then you may as well take the veil," he replied, "for Miles of Louth shall never have you. That I swear."

Lynette sank to the floor, shaking

with a passionate conflict of emotions. "You are cruel, sir, to use me as a weapon in your fight with Miles. You care not a jot for my feelings."

"Indeed I do. I care that you are hungry. Here, take some more meat. It is well-cooked by now."

She was tempted to refuse, but the pangs of hunger were too strong. The hot meat burned her fingers, but she ate her fill while Edgar did the same, then just as she was steeling herself to fend off his advances Edgar lay down on the opposite side of the fire and composed himself for sleep.

I hate him, hate him, hate him! Lynette thought, staring at his turned back. But even as she chanted the words in her mind some treacherous part of her longed for the strength of his arms about her.

She woke first and rose silently, intent on finding a stream where she could wash herself more thoroughly before Edgar stirred. For a moment she watched his sleeping form, noting the way his hair tangled across his forehead. Her hands itched to smooth that dark hair and touch his face, but she thrust the thoughts away and left the cave.

Ahead of her the hills loomed darkly beneath the last of the stars. They looked impassable, so presumably the route would take her and Edgar through the deep pine forests on the lower slopes, but if heaven were kind they might reach their destination that day. What bliss it would be to slide off her horse and know she need not climb into a saddle again until she chose to do so!

Round a flank of the hill, she came suddenly to the top of a slope covered in loose stones. In the valley below, a stream flowed over those stones, with the further hill covered in a brown growth of bracken mixed here and there with the tender bright green of new shoots. The water gleamed dully in the dawn light, enticing her to edge down the slope.

She fell to her knees beside the stream, gasping at the chill of the water as she plunged her hands into it and splashed it on her face. It tasted like nectar in her parched throat and suddenly she longed to immerse herself in it, washing off the dust and grime of five days in the saddle.

Glancing back to the top of the slope to make sure she was unobserved, she threw off her cloak and reached behind her to undo the lacings of her bedraggled tunic. It came off her shoulders and slid to her hips, then to the ground, leaving her in the closely-fitting under-tunic and chemise. Taking off the under-tunic, she sat down to loosen the garters which held her stockings above the knee, and just as her legs were bared to the morning air she heard a sound which made her freeze.

To her left, only a few strides away, a wild-cat stood on a rock, lashing its thick tail as its golden eyes regarded her, unblinking. Lynette heard the low growling in its throat and knew she had no chance if it attacked. She was naked but for her loose shift.

Very slowly, so as not to alarm the animal, she reached for one of her shoes. The thin leather was worn, but it was the nearest thing she had to a weapon. Hardly breathing, she stared at the bared white fangs as the cat hissed at her.

It crouched, bunching itself for the attack. Suddenly Lynette could not bear the tension. She leapt to her feet, screaming, "Edgar!"

Something flashed through the air, startling the wild-cat. A silver glitter thudded within inches of the animal as it turned tail, leaping away up the valley.

Both hands to her mouth, Lynette turned terrified eyes to the slope, down which Edgar came with a litheness not unlike the cat's, descending in a cloud of dust and a tiny avalanche of stones.

"Oh — " Lynette managed, choking

on the dregs of her fright "Edgar!"

"You fool!" he flung at her as he reached the stream. "I have warned you of the dangers in the wild. God's wounds! If I had not come looking for you that lynx would have torn you to pieces."

Lynette was shivering uncontrollably, partly from the cold and partly from reaction. Tears sprang into her eyes at his harshness and she held out her hands in appeal.

"I'm sorry. Edgar — "

He surveyed her with veiled eyes — her dishevelled hair, the grubby shift that clung almost transparently to her tender curves. Suddenly his eyes met hers, bright with fury.

"Get dressed," he growled. "We must be on our way."

Sobs shook her body as she scrambled into her clothes, though she closed her lips to prevent herself from crying aloud. Edgar, ignoring her, retrieved his dagger and thrust it into the sheath at his belt. He was inhuman, she told herself. She had been very much afraid and had needed comfort, not censure. If only he had held her in his arms instead of looking so angry!

"Now come," he said as she pulled on her second shoe. Taking her hand, he half dragged her to the top of the slope and strode ahead of her while she paused to regain her breath.

I hate him! she thought again, but by then she knew that it was untrue. The realisation ripped through her like a sword-thrust — she loved him. Dear heaven, she loved a thief, a robber chieftain, an abductor of women. It was madness, but she could no longer deny her own heart.

5

AS the sun climbed into the sky, they followed a valley which took them further into the uplands, so that bare hills rose on either side, grim and dark beneath a covering of brown heather. Lynette was horrified when they began to climb towards the end of the valley, heading straight for the bleak hilltops.

"Where are we going?" she gasped.

Edgar, riding ahead of her, glanced over his shoulder. "You know where we are going — to the valley."

"But no one lives in these heights! How could they — "

"They manage." He smiled grimly to himself. "You are correct, my lady. Nothing lives here save the eagles and the hawks — and Edgar of the Moor and his people. Do you not like my homeland?"

Wincing beneath the scorn in his voice, Lynette made no reply. She was angry with herself for succumbing to a hopeless passion for this man who was using her as a pawn in his struggle with Miles. He did not care for her — he had made that very clear. Why was her heart foolish enough to open itself to the pain of loving him?

One thing she promised herself — Edgar would never guess from any word or deed of hers that she cared for him. No, that was a secret she would guard with her life.

After a while they reached the top of the climb and the view which spread out before them took Lynette's breath away. Ahead of them stretched a great ocean of heather, rippling over the uneven landscape and marked here and there with a pale outcrop of rock. She had never seen such a place, never guessed that a land so desolate existed.

Drawing rein, Edgar made a wide gesture which encompassed all the wilderness ahead of them. "Behold!" he said in a low voice. "My moors. Welcome to my kingdom, my dear wife. Welcome to the land your people left to us when they took the rest by force of arms."

Lynette said nothing, though she wondered if he disliked her because she was a Norman, one of the conquerors who had disinherited his people.

"So silent?" Edgar said, a wry smile twitching at his mouth. "If I had realised the moors would have that effect on you I would have hurried you here sooner."

"What is it you wish me to say?" Lynette asked dully. "Pray do not play games with me, sir. I am at your mercy. Does it amuse you to torment me?"

"I thought it was the way you expected me to behave," he replied. "No, it does not amuse me, but you set us on this course by naming me barbarian and brigand. I would be gentle with you, if you gave me leave."

Lynette's heart seemed to turn over, but she stared at the horizon fixedly, keeping her face still. If he was gentle, she would melt. She knew it. But she needed to keep her pride, which was all he had left her.

"I doubt that you would know how," she said. "You have amply proved to me that you are no gentle man."

Then if that is the way you would have it so shall it be," Edgar said, reaching to grab the leading rein of her mount. "Spur up, my lady. I will show you the rest of my kingdom."

The black charger leapt forward at a gallop, so that the mare was obliged to follow. Lynette hung on grimly with aching thighs, her braids thumping against her breast and her cloak billowing behind her as they stormed across the heathland at a gallop. Ahead of her, Edgar's dark cloak tossed in the wind that whipped over his moors, but she bit her lips against an urge to plead for him to stop. She had already shown him too much of her weakness.

The moors seemed to go on for ever. Each new crest revealed yet more of the empty land and now they were deep in the heart of it, brown waves rolling on every side, featureless and trackless. It was a mystery how Edgar knew his way.

Eventually he slowed the pace, more for the horses' sake than for hers, and they rode on while the sun climbed to the zenith and began to drop on their left.

Just when Lynette thought she could go no further without food and drink there came, faintly on the cold breeze, the thin cry of a horn — two long notes it sounded, a pause, then another note. She glanced at Edgar, puzzled, and saw him smile to himself.

"We are expected," he said, reaching to unfasten the bronze brooch which secured his cloak at one shoulder. To Lynette's amazement, he swirled the garment and replaced it with the lining outermost, the shaggy grey fur sweeping from his shoulders to cover the flanks of his horse.

"Now you truly look like a barbarian," she remarked.

"Aye. And soon you shall see the great horned helm of my ancestors," he said, looking her up and down. "You should be better dressed for such a home-coming, but it will serve."

As they rode on, Lynette scanned the horizon for signs of a camp, but saw nothing save the heather, the rocks, and a hawk gliding low in the distance. Within a few minutes, however, she began to make out what appeared to be a deep crack in the face of the land and as they drew nearer the crack widened becoming a deep valley. She glimpsed the thick growth of trees on the further side and realised that she was being led down an incline, between two humps of the moor. For a while the flank of the hill shut the valley from sight, then slowly it appeared again, a broad area with woods on either side and green meadows flanking the river which twined across the valley floor.

Gazing with wonder as the view opened out, Lynette flinched when a figure leapt from behind a rock in front of them, revealing itself as the impish form of young Ulf, grinning broadly. He wore a horn slung round his neck.

"My lord!" he greeted Edgar. "You are welcome. And my lady — welcome again."

"Are you watchman for today?" Edgar asked, his voice deep with an affection which surprised Lynette.

"Aye, my lord," Ulf said eagerly. "They sent me to watch this end of the valley, thinking you would come this way."

The lad jumped up to the rock and stood glowing with pride as Lynette followed her husband down the sloping track towards the valley bottom. Just before they reached the trees, Edgar paused and glanced back at her. "How do you like my forest camp?"

Lynette could still hardly believe her eyes. Threads of smoke rising told her that among the woods there were habitations and at the far end of the valley, where a pass seemed to lead to dense forests, she could see the pale shape of a stone tower rising among a mass of other buildings all surrounded by a palisade. The sardonic gleam in Edgar's eyes told her he was amused by her wordlessness.

"This valley — " she said slowly " — is your land?"

"Mine by right of inheritance. It is called Wulfrith's Dale. Wulfrith was my grandfather, and his son Wulfrith was my father." White teeth showed briefly in his dark face as he smiled. "Did I not tell you I was the son of a wolf?"

The lightening of his spirits only caused Lynette to sink deeper into mortification. He had let her prate on at him, calling him brigand, when all the time he had known what waited in his valley.

"You misled me, sir," she said flatly.

"You misled yourself, my lady," he

returned with a laugh, and urged his horse on down the steep path.

Lynette heard the sound of a waterfall and saw it coursing down the hillside to disappear among the trees. As they reached level ground she glimpsed a pool that sparkled deep in the woods with the waterfall splashing down into it. The track followed the course of the river, passing by a mill and finally emerging into sunlight, among the fenced meadows caught glimpses of the wood and turf houses among the trees on either side and occasionally a child and fields cultivated in broad strips. Now Lynette peeped out to watch them curiously.

"The priest Machel led my grandfather to this valley when the Conqueror drove us from our own lands," Edgar said, riding alongside her as the track broadened. "It was hard at first. The land had to be cleared before they could grow crops and they lived on roots and berries — and what they could steal or beg. The Conqueror left us little choice. When he came to the north he burned everything to force a surrender. Many died of starvation, but some found their way to our valley and settled here."

Lynette glanced up at the dark hills which guarded the place and remembered the long ride across the moors. "But you must need goods from outside. It is so far from any market!"

"Not so far. Half a day's ride beyond the valley." He slanted her an apologetic smile. "We came by the back door, the long way, in case of pursuit."

She pulled a face. Had he dragged her through forests and over mountains without need?

"But even the short way has its dangers," Edgar added. "You would need a guide to show you the way."

He was warning her that there was no way of escape, she thought, but beyond an urgent need for news of her father she had no desire to leave him.

She glanced at his strong profile, his skin darkened by wind and sun. The breeze played in strands of his hair and ruffled the wolfskin fur that cloaked him, while at his side his sword hung in its decorated scabbard and the green jewels on the handle of his dagger gleamed. With prickles playing across her skin she considered his long, well-muscled legs and broad shoulders, and the hands which lay lightly on the reins — strong brown hands innocent now of rings, for he had given her the only ring he wore. She turned it on her finger, remembering his hands on her. A soft flush crept into her cheeks as she thought of the coming night when they would be alone in his sleeping chamber. Oh, if only he had come openly to seek her hand, how happy she would be now!

She saw that they were coming to the manor house, where a bend of the river had been diverted to form a deep moat. Beyond it a bank was topped with a wooden palisade. The stone keep lifted two-storeys high above other roofs thatched with heather, and to judge by the size of the courtyard it could provide shelter for all who lived in the valley, and for their livestock, in case of attack.

The hooves rang over the drawbridge and then they were in the courtyard, which reminded Lynette strongly of Braxby. Here chickens scratched and dogs roamed, while around the palisade the barns, cow-sheds and other out-houses grouped. The great hall, built of white-washed logs, backed onto the stone keep, and servants scurried to and fro. The ring of hammer on anvil came clear to Lynette and she smelled the aroma of cooking from the kitchen huts. It was a familiar scene, but not so welcome were the sidelong looks being flung at her. These were Saxons and she was Norman. She sensed hostility in the very air she breathed.

As Edgar dismounted, a huge shaggy hound came from the main house, woofing as it charged at its master, almost bowling him over. Lynette heard him laugh as he patted the dog's black head, while a man came to help her down.

She saw with surprise that it was Ned, grinning widely. She had never thought she would be pleased to see him, but the sight of his familiar and friendly face cheered her.

"You've come far, my lady," he said. "You must be weary."

She smiled faintly at him, but her eyes flicked beyond him to where a young woman stood by the door of the great hall, arms folded across a tunic of brilliant blue and a smile on her lips as she watched Edgar playing with his dog.

"Welcome home, my lord," she said clearly sweeping into a curtsey as Edgar straightened. "All is prepared for your coming."

"Thank you, Johanna," he replied, extending a hand towards Lynette. She placed her own hand on his and allowed herself to be drawn forward; more conscious than ever of her dirty, dishevelled state. Johanna looked immaculate, a silver circlet holding a gossamer veil over hair as pale as moonlight, twisted with ribbons which matched her tunic. At her throat a jewel gleamed and round the hem and sleeves of her gown delicate flowers were embroidered in a rainbow of colours mixed with silver thread. She was the ideal of beauty, Lynette thought with a pang of envy — slender, tall and fair — and in her lovely face glowed eyes of a deep violet, watchful eyes, full of curiosity.

"This is Mistress Johanna," Edgar said. "She is the widow of my uncle."

Long eyelashes veiled those deep blue eyes as Johanna sketched another curtsey. "My lady, welcome. There is food prepared. I shall order a bath to be filled for you."

"Food first," Edgar said with a sidelong smile that made fun of Lynette. "My lady has a healthy appetite."

His fingers held hers impersonally as he led her into the great hall, where the high table had been laid for them anew since it was well past the hour for dinner. Lynette saw the fire on its stone hearth in the centre of the hall, smoke curling up to blacken the rafters and leak through a louvre, but the place differed from her own home in that the walls were hung with painted linen depicting scenes of warfare and country life. Behind the high table, the wall-hanging was dominated by a picture of a huge man, black-bearded, wearing a horned helmet, and on a nearby beam hung what had to be the original of that helmet, made of bronze and brightly polished.

"Wulfrith's helm," Edgar said, seeing her gaze at it.

A servant brought water and towels for them to wash their hands, then they sat side by side at the high table to eat of the food that was brought. Although Lynette was hungry, she found that she could not eat. Strangely, now that they had reached their goal she felt more unsettled than ever. She had expected a rough outlaw camp, not this pleasant manor where Edgar, her beloved brigand, had suddenly turned into a Saxon lord.

Pulling up a stool, Johanna seated herself on Edgar's right and watched as he helped himself to more meat from the platter.

"You have travelled slowly," she said. "We expected you yesterday."

"Aye, it took longer than I planned," Edgar replied. "My lady is not used to such far journeying. But we are safely come. I trust you will show my lady her duties and help her settle among us."

"Indeed I shall," Johanna said, casting a smiling glance at Lynette. "But you took us all by surprise, my lord. We had not expected you to return with a wife."

"I have always told you I should wed when I found a lady to please me," he said levelly.

Lynette's heart gave a curious lurch.

Did she please him? Then she jumped and paled when Edgar abruptly turned to her.

"You are not eating. Is the food not to your taste?"

"The food is — is excellent," Lynette faltered. "But I fear I am too weary to appreciate it."

If they had been alone she might also have said that she was afraid, feeling unwelcome among strangers who distrusted anyone of Norman blood, and unsure even of her husband. While they travelled together she had thought she was beginning to understand him, but now he, too, seemed like a stranger and she was all the more aware of being a hostage in a hostile land.

She fancied that she saw his face soften, but before he could reply Ned came hurrying from the far end of the hall to bend a knee briefly before them.

"Your pardon, my lord," he said breathlessly. "I beg you come and speak to the people. There is unrest among them." His glance slid across Lynette, telling her that she was the cause of the unrest.

Edgar flung down his napkin and rose to his feet, his face stormy. "What nonsense is this? Tell them I shall come immediately, Ned. God's teeth, can a man not be allowed to dine in peace? My lady — forgive me. Johanna will show you to your chamber. Refresh yourself and rest. I shall soon settle this uproar."

He strode from the chamber, the shaggy black hound at his heels, leaving Lynette and Johanna alone but for the shadowy figures of servants near the screens which separated the pantry and the buttery from the main hall.

"Will you come with me, my lady?" Johanna said softly, a half smile curving her lovely mouth. "You look weary and travel-stained. It is no way for a bride to appear before her husband."

"My husband knows what caused my lack of grooming," Lynette replied, irritated by the implied criticism.

"Of course. I expect you wore your finest for him while he was courting you and when you wed. Let us restore his bride to her full beauty. It will please him."

Her manner was all sympathy and understanding, but something about this silver-fair woman grated on Lynette's nerves. The widow of Edgar's uncle she might be, but she was not much older than Lynette herself. By rights she should have stayed in her husband's home. Lynette wondered what kind of relationship Edgar and Johanna had shared, but her suspicions were too painful and she thrust them aside. Edgar was now married and out of Johanna's reach. Lynette promised herself she would make sure he stayed that way.

Sweeping aside the wall-hangings, Johanna revealed an inner chamber, but then she stepped to a curtained doorway and led Lynette out into the courtyard beside the hall. Stairs climbed up the outside of the keep, covered by a wooden canopy.

"When Edgar ordered the building of the keep," Johanna said as she trod carefully up the covered stairway, "he had chambers set aside for his own use. Edgar likes his privacy, at times, though he does not always sleep in the keep."

Then where does he sleep? Lynette wondered, but to have asked such a question would have revealed her suspicion.

Partway up the tower, a door opened off, though the stairs went on to the flat roof which could be useful for defence. The upper floor of the keep was divided into three — a large storage chamber for dry goods and two adjoining rooms which formed a bed-chamber and private sitting room.

As Johanna showed her into the bed-chamber, Lynette rubbed her perspiring hands on her tunic. The room was much larger than her own chamber at home and it held the grandest bed she had ever seen — a canopied, curtained bed boasting pillows covered in finest linen, linen sheets, fine wool blankets and a fur rug for a coverlet. In the fireplace built into the wall, logs blazed and in front of them stood a tall wooden tub, faintly steaming.

A shaft of hope sprang into Lynette's nervous thoughts. If she were clean and well-groomed perhaps Edgar would look at her in a different way. He was a man, after all, and if she could be sweet and tender with him he might respond.

"I will save you from the draughts," Johanna said, moving to close the shutters across the narrow window opening. "At this time of year the air still strikes chill, even if the sun is warm."

In half-light aided by the flickering fire Lynette glanced at the chests by the walls, the fox-pelts scattered on the floor boards and the poles from which clothes could be hung.

"It will be more comfortable than sleeping in caves," Johanna said.

"Yes." Her voice came out choked with apprehension. "Yes, indeed we shall be pleased to have arrived home at last, my lord and I. Thank you, Johanna. I think I can manage now."

"But you must let me help you," Johanna said, beginning to unlace Lynette's tunic. "Edgar will have to see that you are given a maid. Of course I have my own serving woman, but I need her services. As thegn's wife you must have a maid to attend you. Oh — a thegn, that is a baron, as you Normans call it."

"I know." Lynette thought that if Johanna did not leave her alone she would scream, but she bit back her nerves and allowed the other girl to help her undress as far as her chemise.

She climbed the short ladder and felt for the foot-holds on the inside of the tub, carefully letting herself down into the warm water. A sweet scent assailed her nostrils as the steam rose and she dipped in up to her shoulders, luxuriating in the wonder of a bath when she had begun to think she would never be clean again.

Over the rim of the tub, Johanna regarded her with a smile that was mildly ironic. "You had best give me your chemise, too, my lady. Clean garments await you."

"Oh?" Lynette said in surprise.

"Ned told us you left your home somewhat — suddenly, shall we say? Edgar sent word that we were to prepare a new wardrobe for you."

Lynette bent her head, unbraiding her hair as she furiously wondered how much Johanna knew of her abduction and enforced marriage, though she was pleased that Edgar had anticipated her needs.

"Of course, Edgar is known to be impetuous," Johanna said. "Do I gather you came unwillingly?"

"Is that what you were told?" Lynette asked cautiously.

Johanna's laughter filled the dimly-lit chamber. "It was a fine tale. Imagine Edgar having to abduct his own wife

153

to make her come to heel! What a blow that must have been to his pride. But I know how you must have felt. I, too, was given in marriage without my consent, though I vow that Edgar is more of a prize than was his uncle. He is young and handsome. My husband was past fifty, grey and crippled with rheumatism. He had sons older than I. But heaven was kind and freed me after three years."

Soaping herself down, Lynette felt vaguely shocked at hearing such words. It was a woman's place to wed whomever her father chose, whether she liked it or not. She herself had never questioned that she must marry Miles.

Miles! Stricken, she realised she had hardly given him a thought for days, save to fling his name in Edgar's face. What was Miles doing now — was he searching for her, heart-broken?

As she pulled off her shift and laid it dripping, over the rim of the tub, Johanna sat down on the bed.

"Tell me," she said with a confidential air, "what did you do to make Edgar lose his head over you? No Norman has ever before come to this valley. There are those who say you are a spy and will bring enemies to burn our crops."

"Are Saxons so faint-hearted they fear one woman?" Lynette said scornfully.

"They fear what you represent. Do you ask me to believe it was your beauty that won the heart of Edgar of the Moor?" Her tone said that could not possibly be the answer.

Annoyed, Lynette began to soap her hair. "You had best ask him. He is the only one who can answer that question."

"Or are you rich?" Johanna persisted. "It is certain that Edgar needs more income than the valley brings him — and the prince his patron has no lands to give away as rewards. Are you a great heiress, my lady? Did Prince Henry give you to Edgar?"

"I fear not." A mischievous idea

of how she could still Johanna's acid tongue occurred to Lynette. The scented bath had worked miracles for her spirit as she leaned on the rim of the tub, looking Johanna in the eye. "The truth is, Mistress Johanna, that my lord and I met when he rescued me after I fell from my horse. I was betrothed to another knight, but since Sir Edgar could not bear to think of my marrying another man he carried me off with him and brought me here. It is true that I was at first unwilling, but he has taught me to appreciate him. What woman could resist my lord when he is determined?"

Anger flashed in Johanna's eyes. She stood up abruptly, her hands clenched. "I have eyes and ears. He does not look at you as a lover does. I do not believe he would have risked the safety of this valley for a momentary whim."

"You said yourself he is impetuous," Lynette reminded her.

"Not where Wulfrith Dale is concerned! There is some other reason. There must be! And — " her face cleared as the thought occurred to her " — if he abducted you, then you are not his wife. He has taken you as his mistress!"

"No!" Lynette cried, turning pale. "We were wed. See — I wear his ring."

Johanna glanced at the ring with its black stone, her face taut with fury. "That is no proof. How could he wed you in the forest?"

"We were married by the priest Machel!"

"Machel!" The violet eyes narrowed. "The hermit?"

"Yes. Three days ago — and three nights," she could not resist adding defiantly.

Coming close to the tub, Johanna peered into her face. "I still do not believe he loves you. Why did he marry you? What lands do you bring for dowry? What wealth?"

"None." Lynette found herself shivering in the cooling water, mainly from nerves. She did not know for sure why Edgar had married her.

"No lands?"

"I am heiress to one small manor, that is all."

Scorn twisted Johanna's mouth. "One manor! Do you actually believe it was your beauty that swayed him? You are no beauty, my lady. And red hair is suited only to witches. Where lies your manor? Is it rich in produce?"

"No more than any other," Lynette said faintly.

"Our sheep produce fine wool, but Braxby is not — "

"Braxby!" It was a whisper. Johanna's eyes widened as she backed away. "So that is the answer!" Suddenly she laughed and spun around as if dancing. "Braxby! My dear Lady Lynette — did you really think it was passion that moved him? Oh, you are funnier than a jester!"

Her silver laughter bubbled from her, while Lynette stared in dismay from her tub.

"What is so amusing about Braxby?" she asked in a hushed voice. "It is one small manor. He did not marry me for that."

"Oh, but he did!" Calming herself, Johanna walked softly across the room and patted Lynette's bare arm. "Forgive me. I did not intend to make mock of you. But you are so innocent! Braxby — Braxby lies in the very heart of the lands which once belonged to Edgar's grandfather. Many times I have heard Edgar swear he would get possession of it again, one way or another. Well, he has found his way, has he not? Without even a drop of blood being shed, he has regained his ancestral land. The Normans took it from Wulfrith; now Edgar takes a Norman. Check and mate, I believe. Check and mate!" Trying to contain her delight, she glanced around the chamber. "Oh, dear, the stupid girl has forgotten to bring towels. I will send her to you."

Taking all Lynette's clothes with her,

she left the room, still laughing to herself.

Lynette stared at the closed door, despair burning behind her eyes. She tried to tell herself Johanna was wrong, but all too clearly she recalled her first meeting with Edgar. He had frowned when she told him she was betrothed to Miles, but when she mentioned that her home was Braxby he had been furious. Now she knew that it was because his enemy, by marrying her, would come into possession of the land he regarded as his own. Of course he would not allow that. It was because of Braxby that he had plotted to abduct her and force her into marriage — because of Braxby!

And she had been foolish enough to believe that he might care for her, if only a little. She had actually thought that love might grow between them.

The misery she had been hiding for days suddenly welled up and she laid her head on her arm, sobbing bitterly.

6

"MY lady?" A timid voice and a scratching at the door broke into Lynette's distress. "I've brought your towels, my lady."

"Then come in!" Lynette cried. "Must I stand here and — " She stopped, for despite the half-light she saw that the young serving girl who came in looked as unhappy as she herself felt, with great brown eyes swollen and red-rimmed. She also looked fearful.

"Hold the towel for me," Lynette said as gently as she could when her throat ached from weeping.

The girl obeyed, averting her face as Lynette climbed from the tub and wrapped the thick linen around her, taking another towel to cocoon her hair. She turned to find the maid staring at her open-mouthed.

"Well, child?"

"You — you speak English!"

Sighing, Lynette sat down on the great bed. "I was born in England. Are you surprised, too, that I have only one head? Don't be afraid. Tell me your name."

"It's — it's Acha, my lady."

"And why have you been weeping?"

"The lady Johanna was angry with me for forgetting the towels. I did bring them, but I heard you talking and — "

"And you went away again because you were terrified of me?" Lynette guessed. "Acha — look at me. I am the same as you, even though I am a Norman. Look — five fingers on my hand, five toes on my feet, even scratches on my skin from riding through briars. Am I so frightening?"

Acha shook her head, her brown eyes reminding Lynette of a new-born calf. "Has Lady Johanna been angry with you, too?"

"No," Lynette said with a weary

laugh. "No, child, I weep because — oh, because I am weak and foolish and dream too many dreams. I weep because I am a woman and the world was made for men. Some day, perhaps, you will understand."

The maid regarded her in a puzzled way, pulling at the long dark hair that straggled down her tunic. "They say you will bring evil to the valley," she said.

"Who says this?"

"Harald, and Eric. But Ned stood against them, and so did Ulf. Ulf told me you were — beautiful."

"Did he?" Lynette said with a sad smile. "That was kind."

"I thought all Normans were ugly, and cruel," Acha told her. "They drove us from our homes and burned our houses and all the land, though that was before I was born. Harald said that soldiers would come to take you from Sir Edgar and punish us."

"Then Harald is a donkey," Lynette said. "No one will come after me."

Edgar had made sure of that, she thought bitterly. Perhaps he would send word to her father, advising him of their marriage, and when her father died Edgar would send a steward to manage the Braxby estate and collect the rents and dues for him. But it was not the revenue he wanted, it was ownership of the land. The thought made fresh tears well in her eyes. It would not have been so bad if he had been honest, but he had led her to believe that concern for her well-being had moved him.

"Don't cry, my lady," Acha said, awkwardly touching Lynette's shoulder. "My lord will come soon. He's telling them off this very minute."

"Is he?" Lynette said, amused and yet touched by the child's attempts to comfort her.

"I was down there listening behind a tree when Lady Johanna caught me," Acha confided. "I heard him say that you were his wife for good or ill and if they didn't like it they could all leave the valley and he'd farm it himself."

Brave words, Lynette thought, when none of the peasants had anything beyond the valley and would have to turn outlaw if they left their homes. Of course Edgar would speak for her; by doing so he protected himself.

At that moment the door crashed open to reveal her husband. Frowning blackly, he strode into the room while Lynette stood up, clutching her towel around her, and Acha backed away mumbling something about emptying the tub.

"Leave it," Edgar growled. "I'll use the water myself."

Bobbing a curtsey, Acha began to sidle towards the door.

"Wait!" Lynette said sharply. "Acha — bring me some clothes, please."

Acha stared at her blankly, then lifted a hand and pointed to one of the chests beneath the window. "They're all in there, my lady."

"Oh — thank you."

The maid left, closing the door

quietly behind her. Ignoring Edgar, Lynette made for the chest, but he strode ahead of her and placed a booted foot on the lid, leaning on his knee with a challenge in his eyes.

"Why bother to dress, my lady? Rest yourself while I bathe."

Lynette faced him squarely, her head flung up and spots of scarlet burning on her cheeks. "And then, my lord?"

"Then you shall pay your wifely dues to me," Edgar growled. "It is time, and past time. My people are uneasy because I have brought a Norman to their secret valley. I have been arguing on your behalf this past hour. You owe me some recompense."

"I owe you nothing!" Lynette spat.

She watched in growing apprehension as he slowly unbuckled his sword and laid it across the chest. He tossed off his mantle and undid his belt, his eyes on hers, then suddenly reached for her. As Lynette flinched away, he caught an end of the towel which bound her hair and tore it from her, staring at the flowing masses of red-gold that tumbled damply round her shoulders and almost to her waist.

"Great God!" he muttered under his breath, catching her in his arms with his face buried in her hair.

Her mind rebelled but her treacherous body responded as his lips found the tender place beneath her ear and pressed kisses down her throat. He does not want me, she reminded herself frantically while her pulses jumped in rising ecstasy. He wants Braxby, and sons for Braxby!

"My lady!" he breathed, kissing her shoulder. "My sweet lady!"

Lynette's mind swam. She felt the towel begin to slip. Almost she gave in to the magnetic power of him, wanting him to touch her and caress her, not caring why he did it, but the shreds of her pride remained even while her flesh quivered beneath his hands. She must not give in. She must not! Check and mate, Johanna had said. Well, truly she was checked, but so was Edgar:

there would be no mating if she could prevent it.

Edgar lifted his head, his eyes blazing into hers. "Are you thinking now of Sir Miles?" he asked hoarsely.

"Yes!" She drew a deep, shuddering breath as she flung the lie into his face. "I have told you — I shall always think of Miles!"

Dark blood made his face savage as he thrust her away. She clutched at the towel, wrapping it securely about her, and stood trembling as Edgar threw open the lid of the chest, sending his sword to clatter on the floor.

"Take your clothes," he growled. "I shall not act as proxy for another man. Take them!"

Keeping her burning face averted, Lynette bent over the chest, gathering what garments she needed. She held them against her like a shield while she backed away to the door which led into the adjoining room. As she reached the safety of the further chamber she heard Edgar swear viciously, and then the door was closed.

Lynette stood trembling, wishing she had never even heard the name of Edgar of the Moor. Young Acha showed more concern than he did. Oh, if only he had been kind!

The sound of splashing from the next room told her that Edgar was washing himself with vigour. She moved away from the door and stood by the fire in the barely-furnished room, pulling on a clean cotton chemise. The under-tunic with its tight fitting sleeves fastened with a drawstring round her neck and over it went the super-tunic, cut with a V-neck and full sleeves. The lacings at the back caused her a struggle and she wished she had kept Acha with her to help, then finally she sat down to pull on the linen stockings and tie them with garters above her knees.

To her surprise the garments fitted reasonably well. Someone must have described her with great accuracy. The over-tunic was a shade of apple green, though plain and unembroidered — there had obviously been no time for fancy work.

She sat by the fire, on the bare floorboards covered in rushes, and tried to get some of the tangles out of her hair, using her fingers in place of a comb. Late afternoon sunlight slanted in a dusty ray through the window-opening and from the courtyard below came the sounds of the servants about their work.

Lynette looked about her, at the tapestry-work stools and the table on which a chess-set stood waiting for players. In one corner a dusty harp leaned and another chest shone with painted colours as the sun caught on it. How pleasant it must be to have a private room to escape from the communal life of the great hall. If only she and Edgar had been happily wed she could have enjoyed sitting with him here in the evening, perhaps playing and singing for him in the quiet time before they repaired to bed.

The connecting door opened without

warning and Edgar stood on the threshold — a strange Edgar, the sight of whom brought her to her feet, wide-eyed. Gone was the short black tunic and in its place he wore a sweeping robe dyed dark red from the blackberry plant and embroidered lavishly with gold thread at neck, hem and wide-flowing cuffs. With jewels at his belt and neatly-combed hair he might have been taken for a wealthy Norman lord.

His eyes raked over her, glittering coldly, and he strode to the painted chest, undoing the leather bands that bound it. As he opened the lid, Lynette saw the treasure there — the glow of jewels and the gleam of gold. He took a few items from the chest and turned to her.

"These belonged to my mother," he said. "Wear them, as befits my wife. I wish my people to see their mistress in her splendour tonight, having seen her tired and dusty."

Lynette stared at the glitter in his

hand — rings and bracelets, a slender girdle decorated with emeralds, and a gold circlet for her hair.

"Whatever lies between us when we two are alone," Edgar said, "we must behave as turtle-doves in front of my people. I beg you, my lady, though you hate me, do this for me. In Wulfrith's Dale there are no serfs, no villeins, only free men who give their allegiance to me from choice. They are suspicious of us, but their fears will ease if they think us united."

He was actually pleading with her. Aware that she had some power over him at last, Lynette lifted her eyes to his face. "Why should I do that for you? Do you expect me to play a part to make your life easy when you have taken my life and turned it over?"

"Your life will be much harder if you dispute with me in public," he assured her. "I cannot stay forever in the valley. My duties call me back to Prince Henry's side, and since you cannot go with me — " He left the rest unspoken, but she had a vision of herself left alone in the dale, the only Norman among Saxons who mistrusted her.

"It is a pity," she said tautly, "that you did not give the matter more thought before now."

"Aye." He sighed heavily, his mouth grim. "I had forgotten that here the war goes on, though outside our peoples are learning to live in peace. I acknowledge the fault, but what would you have me do?"

"Let me go!"

"I cannot do that! You are my wife!"

"We could amend that mistake," she said coldly. "Let me go, my lord. Let me return to my true betrothed."

"Never!" Edgar vowed. "No, never. Forget Miles of Louth. You are mine, in the eyes of God, and mine you shall stay."

Wistfully, Lynette wished he meant it as it sounded, but she knew that it was Braxby he was thinking of, and his hatred of Miles.

She lowered her eyes, saying in a voice that shook, "Very well, my lord. I shall behave — in public — like a good, obedient wife." Flinging up her head, she added fiercely, "But not for your sake. Since I am obliged to stay here I shall take pleasure in showing your people that not all Normans are cruel tyrants. It shall be my quest in life to heal the breech that remains here."

"Then at last we have something to agree upon," Edgar said in an undertone. Laying his gifts to her on the low table, he walked to the door, the red-robe flowing softly round his long legs. "I shall come for you when supper is prepared," he said as he left.

As the sun went down over the far end of the valley, sinking towards the dark, heather-clad hills, Lynette sat by the fire and stared at the flames. Jewels gleamed on her hands, her wrists and at her waist, while the gold circlet held a filmy veil over her hair. She had found a comb and twined her braids with yellow ribbons, also discovering a dark green mantle that fell softly behind her, but though she knew she looked her best her heart was bleak: There was nothing any more but the prospect of a life as mistress of Wulfrith's Dale — a name so alien she could hardly pronounce it. And that life would be empty.

When Edgar came in, she rose gracefully to her feet and stood silent under his scrutiny. Tiny nerves on her skin jumped as his gaze moved slowly over her, but she kept her head high and her face impassive.

"You do me honour," he said quietly. "Truly you look the part of lady of the Dale."

"As you wished me to look," Lynette replied.

"Your beauty outshines any jewels I might give you," he said.

For a moment Lynette's heart softened, but with an effort she turned it back to ice. "You learned the game of flattery well at King William's court, my lord. But you said you disliked it.

I, too, can live without pretty lies. Let us get on with our play acting, if we must."

"My people are waiting to see you," he said with a little bow, his lip curling slightly. "Let me show them my lovely — and docile — bride."

She gave him her hand and allowed him to lead her down the covered stairway to the courtyard where Ned waited with her grey mare decked with spring flowers. Edgar lifted her to sit sideways across the saddle and walked beside her, dark and arrogant in his flowing robe, as Ned led the mare towards the gate, accompanied by stares from faces peeping from the out-houses.

Beyond the gate, on the other side of the drawbridge, the people of the dale had gathered in an expectant crowd, men, women and children murmuring together. The sun shone full in Lynette's eyes and it seemed to her as though the people were one mass of humanity with many heads all turned to stare at her.

As the murmuring stopped, Lynette squinted through the sun's brightness, trying to pick out faces and hoping her embarrassment was not evident, though a semblance of shyness would not be amiss in a bride. She heard the silence spread until there was nothing to be heard but a lark pouring out his evening song from the sky far above.

Edgar took a deep breath and his voice rang out across the waiting crowd:

"When Wulfrith my grandfather found this valley, more than thirty years ago, he welcomed all men who came in peace. Your fathers and grandfathers swore the oath of fealty to him, and you have all taken an oath to me, as his heir. Now in peace comes the lady Lynette, wife of Edgar of the Moor. You will honour her, for my sake."

Although no one spoke there was a shuffling in the crowd and Lynette sensed the fears and doubts which ran through the people. They respected

Edgar as their rightful lord, but they were suspicious of this Norman he had brought among them.

"Let her speak for herself!" someone called, and a mutter of agreement rose.

Edgar looked up at Lynette, his expression pleading with her not to let him down. "Speak to them, my lady, in their own language."

"What shall I say?" she breathed, horrified.

"Anything that will set their minds at rest."

She looked up, just as the sun touched the rim of the hills, spreading shadows across the valley. A hush had fallen as the people waited.

"My friends — " she began, and paused, flushing, as someone laughed derisively. Then, remembering that she was a Norman lady, she lifted her chin and spoke from her heart. "I hope you will become my friends, all of you. It is true that I come of Norman stock, but I was born and raised in your England

and know no other home. I come as a stranger, save for the love I bear your lord, but I would extend that love to you all, if you allow me."

She could not go on for the tears that choked her. She was telling the truth, if only they would believe it:

"A nice touch," Edgar said under his breath. "The tears of a lovely woman would melt the stoniest heart."

The sun dazzled through her tears, making his face indistinct, but the sarcasm of his tone told her enough.

"*Waes Hael!*" a young voice cried. "*Waes Hael* for the lady Lynette, flower of the Normans! *Waes Hael* for our thegn's wife!"

Out from the crowd a slim figure darted and Lynette recognised the boy Ulf as he ran to kneel in front of her, his face lifted in a bright smile. He leapt to his feet and presented her with a spoon he had carved himself.

Driven by something outside herself, Lynette laid a hand on Edgar's shoulder and gestured for him to help her down from the saddle. He took her by the waist and lifted her to the ground, a question in his eyes.

"Thank you, Ulf," she said softly to the youth, and reached to kiss his brow: Whether it was the right or the wrong thing to do, it was what she felt — sheer gratitude that one person, at least, welcomed her unreservedly.

A moment later she knew it had been the right thing, for the whole crowd began to move forward, a few at a time, to give her the Saxon greeting of '*Waes Hael*' and to lay simple gifts at her feet. Most of the people regarded her with a veiled wariness. They were prepared to accept her, for the moment, but she knew they were far from trusting her. It was, however, a beginning, thanks to Ulf, who stood by with a grin nearly splitting his face in two.

Her own smile had begun to feel stiff when one of the oldest women hobbled forward clutching something wrapped in sacking.

"My husband made this, many years

ago," she croaked. "We weren't blessed, but you and your lord may have better luck."

Lynette's heart seemed to jump into her throat as the sacking came off and the old woman laid at her feet — a cradle, a baby's cradle. Now that she looked, many of the gifts were symbols of fertility, from the loaf to the doll made out of straw. The people were attempting to make sure she provided them with an heir.

A cloud seemed to cross her vision. She was suddenly weary and aware that she had hardly eaten all day. She would have fallen in a swoon had not Edgar stepped up, his arm coming firmly round her as he pressed her to his side. His voice seemed to reach her from a long distance.

"We thank you," he said. "We thank you all. But my lady is fatigued after our long journey. Come, my love."

Her senses swooped near to oblivion as she was swept off the ground into Edgar's arms, her head resting on his shoulder as he carried her back across the drawbridge and into the courtyard. As he climbed the covered stairs her head began to clear and she saw the forbidding aspect of his face, a frown creasing his brow and his mouth stern.

As he laid her on the bed, she asked faintly, "Did I disgrace you?"

Edgar straightened himself and laughed sharply. "Disgrace me? No, my lady, you played the part to perfection — the tears and the melting weakness. Your talents amaze me."

She closed her eyes against the fresh tears that stung them, shutting out the sight of his mocking face. "It was what you wished me to do — win them over."

"Aye. But that you should play it so well — that I had not expected. It was a touch of genius to speak so tenderly of the love you bear me. God's teeth, you near convinced even me!"

The contempt in his voice whipped through her like a flail of briars. She sat up and faced him defiantly. "I imagined I was speaking of Miles!"

There, she had wounded him in return. Edgar's eyes turned cold as mountain lakes, but before he could reply a horn blew in the courtyard, announcing the readiness of supper.

He reached out for her hand, his fingers painfully tight on her flesh. "Then continue your self-delusion, my lady," he said through his teeth. "We have still to endure supper."

The great hall buzzed with voices as Edgar led her from behind the drapes at the rear. The household members lined the outer sides of two long tables, while at the high table the fair Johanna waited. Lynette took her place at Edgar's left hand, with Johanna on his right, and the kitchen staff brought in the food and drink.

The main dishes proved to be grouse done in a tasty sauce and fish caught from the river, though there were also soups, stews and pottages, and cakes and sweetmeats made with honey. The cooks had gone to a deal of trouble to prepare a suitable home-coming feast for their lord and his bride.

At first the sight of the food made Lynette feel slightly sick, but when she had eaten a few mouthfuls the nausea went away and she realised it had been caused by hunger. After all, she had not eaten properly during the journey and that noon she had been able only to pick at her dinner. Now her healthy young body demanded replenishment and she was able to do full justice to the meal by ignoring the soreness of her heart.

To her surprise the evening passed quietly. Edgar gave her half his attention, helping her to the choicest cuts of the meat and being polite as a husband ought, and the rest of the time he conversed with Johanna about the running of the household, drawing Lynette's attention to matters which would be her concern in the future.

My lady was telling me a most delightful tale," Johanna said as the second course came to an end and the wine goblets were refilled. She sent Lynette a flashing smile before turning her violet eyes to Edgar's face. "It told of a brave knight who came to a lady's rescue and was so enamoured of her that he whisked her away from under the nose of her betrothed and carried her away to the forest, where they were married by a priestly hermit." She laughed softly. "An absorbing story, don't you agree, my lord?"

Lynette held her breath. She feared that Edgar would be angry or, even worse, pour withering scorn on her.

He stared into his wine, turning the cup in his fingers. "Some might find it so."

"It would make a wonderful ballad if some skilful minstrel could make a tune for it," Johanna said. "Though I fear it is hardly realistic. Men sing and make poetry about love, but in the real world marriages are made only for profit, as I know all too well. Your uncle would not have wed me had I not brought excellent lands as my dowry."

Edgar was slouched in his chair, rings glittering on the brown hand that toyed with the goblet, but Lynette saw him glance at her from his eye corner and knew that beneath the lazy pose he was tense as a wild-cat when it crouched ready to spring. Hardly daring to breathe, she waited to hear his reply.

"My uncle," he said slowly, "wed you also for your own self, my dear Johanna. And now that he is dead you have full control of your dowry lands. Many a man would be glad to have you."

Bafflement showed on Johanna's face, as if she did not understand how he had turned the conversation to her own prospects.

"Many a man would be glad to have my lands," she amended. "I am wise in the ways of the world, my lord. But your lady would have me believe that there are men who would take a wife for love alone."

"My lady and I know what lies

between us," Edgar replied quietly, laying a hand over Lynette's.

Her skin vibrated to his touch and her hand trembled like a captive bird as his strong brown fingers closed round it. His warmth made her realise how cold she was, cold with dread of the coming night when she must again suffer her inner struggle with her love for him.

Johanna's narrowed gaze remained on their joined hands for a moment, as if she did not know what to believe, and Lynette stifled a sob of bitter-laughter. Edgar's talents at playing the fond spouse matched her own.

"When I return to the court," he said, "I shall ask the king to find you a husband, Johanna. Someone young and handsome — you have had enough of old men I venture."

"Aye," she said drily. "I would rather pay the fine than wed with old age again. But he will have to be a man among men, my lord. I have heard tell of one whose fame interests me, and they say he is as comely as he is brave. If you could persuade the king to give me Miles of Louth for husband I would be well content."

At the sound of Miles's name, Edgar's hand tightened around Lynette's so strongly that she nearly cried out in pain.

"Since you have wed a Norman," Johanna was saying, "I may seek in that direction — myself."

Impatience drew Edgar's brows together and he released Lynette as if her hand had suddenly become red-hot. "If you have heard aught of Miles of Louth," he said roughly, "then you know he has no love for me, nor for any Saxon."

Johanna blinked, long eyelashes sweeping her milk-pale cheeks. "I spoke thoughtlessly, my lord. Forgive me. In my foolishness I saw you as twin stars, glaring balefully from either side of the sky, both equally bright, and since the one is out of my reach I thought to — "

"Enough!" Edgar exclaimed, slamming his hand down on the table so that the goblets jumped. Two spots of wine spread like blood on the white cloth, drawing Lynette's eyes. It seemed like an omen. Miles and Edgar. Edgar and Miles. Must one of them die before this enmity ended?

He leapt from his chair, turning to draw Lynette to her feet. "Come, my lady. It is time we were abed."

Calling a general goodnight to the hall, he swept Lynette away through the curtains and into the starlit courtyard, where he stopped to take a deep breath of the cold night air, as if to calm himself. His hand still clasped Lynette's, though he appeared to have forgotten her.

"Even in my own home he haunts me now," he said under his breath, and suddenly swung round to look at Lynette. "Well, my lady, so you have been chattering about this man who was once your betrothed?"

"I have not!" Lynette gasped.

"No? Then indeed his fame spreads far. You see, you are not the only lady who sighs for him."

"I blame no feminine heart for melting before him," she said steadily. "Miles is the king's champion, true and valiant, brave in battle and tender in love — and honest. The dark and secretive ways of brigands would be beneath him, unlike some who — "

His grip hardened until she feared her bones would crack and she was driven to breathe, "Sir! Please — "

Edgar bent over her, his eyes glowing in the darkness of his face. "You must expect me to be angry when you question my honour," he said softly, and turned for the stairs. Sensing her reluctance to climb with him to the bed-chamber, he added over his shoulder, "Have no fear, my lady. You shall sleep safe from my attentions."

The bed-chamber was lit by rush-lights flickering on the chests. Having conducted her there, Edgar bowed to her and touched his lips to the hand he had so recently bruised.

"I leave you to your dreams of the valiant Sir Miles," he said. "May they keep you warm through the night."

The ice of his smile smote her like a blow in the ribs, then he turned on his heel and was gone.

Lynette stood quite still, not believing that he would leave her in that way, but the door remained closed and the keep was utterly silent. She told herself she was relieved — yes, glad that he had finally decided to leave her in peace. But the room seemed suddenly very empty and the pain inside her wrenched at her heart. Dear heaven, why did she care so much? Why?

7

WHEN it was still dark, Lynette was disturbed by sounds of movement and voices in the courtyard. She leapt out of bed and threw back the shutters, peering through the narrow embrasure at the flare of torches below. Horses pranced in the flickering light, and cloaked figures moved around tightening girths and checking the lashed bundles on the pack-horses.

She saw Edgar stride out from the shadows, an unmistakable tall figure with his heavy cloak flapping round him. He was leaving the valley! Sudden fear of being left alone made her take up a loose robe and rush to the door, fastening the garment around her as she fled barefoot down the dark stairs.

"Edgar!" she cried.

The company paused to stare at the

sight of their mistress in a night robe, with her long hair flying. Edgar swung round in surprise, his face hidden from her by a torch which blazed behind him, and came to where she stood on the edge of the circle of light.

"My lady?" he said politely.

"Take me with you!" Lynette begged, laying her hands on his chest. He was dressed in black again, she noted absently. "Please — do not leave me!"

Taking her by the arm, he drew her further into the shadows, out of the hearing of his men. "You know you cannot come with me. A wife must stay and care for her people in her husband's absence. I ride to join Prince Henry's household."

"I know, but — but his wife may need a lady in waiting. I would gladly — "

"The prince is unwed, as yet." Impatience edged his voice. "Do you think me a fool? If I take you to court you will seek out Sir Miles. Do not attempt to blind me with soft pleas at this late hour. You must stay here, and I must go."

"Yes." She bit her lip, looking down at the ground between them to hide her tears. "But take care, my lord. If you should meet Sir Miles — "

"Are you afraid I will kill him?" he asked sardonically.

Lynette lifted her face. "Oh, why is there such enmity between you? Must one of you die because you are both too proud to make peace? Miles is kind and honourable. He would forgive you, if only — "

"The time is long past for that. Too much now lies between us. I have abducted and defiled his betrothed, have I not?"

The cold earth beneath her feet sent clammy fingers to chill her entire body and she shuddered convulsively. "I would tell him I came willingly. I swear I would!"

"You would do that? To ensure his safety? God's eyes, is it such a boundless love you have for him?"

Not for him, she wanted to cry. For you! It is your safety I care about, my dearest lord. But the words would not come, though tears burst from her eyes and dripped down her cheeks.

"So weep for him!" Edgar said roughly. "I am flattered that you are so certain I shall be the victor. Maybe, when he and I finally meet in combat, it will be Edgar of the Moor who lies vanquished. Then will all your prayers be answered, my lady."

He began to turn away, but paused and looked back at her. "Perhaps you should kiss me, since my men are watching. They will expect us to take tender farewells."

Stepping near to him, Lynette slid her arms round his neck and reached up on tiptoe to touch her lips to his with all the love and longing in her. She felt Edgar stiffen in surprise, then his arms swept round her, pressing her close to the length of his body as his mouth possessed hers with angry passion. Bent like a pliant willow against him, Lynette felt the heat of him flood through the thin robe she wore, turning her body to fire. Her fingers tangled in his hair as her lips parted beneath his and for the first time she returned his kiss with equal passion.

When he released her mouth she leaned helplessly against him, supported by his circling arms, and heard his heart thudding while his breath came hoarse in her ear.

"Though you promise me heaven," he whispered fiercely, "I shall kill him, or be killed in the attempt."

He left her so suddenly that she swayed and leaned weakly against the nearest wall, the woven strips of wood rough against her cheek. Through a glitter of tears she watched Edgar step up to his saddle and ride away through the gate followed by five other horsemen and a string of three pack-animals.

A sob dredged up from the centre of her being. He had thought she was offering herself to him in order to save Miles from harm. And how could she blame him when she had so often flung Miles's name at him?

Shivering in the chill, she realised the servants were beginning to stir, leaving their pallets in the hall in the pre-dawn darkness to make up the fires and prepare for the coming day. She turned quietly back to the keep, hugging herself to try to stay warm, and stopped when a pale shape materialised by the side door of the great hall.

"You think you have him now?" Johanna's voice floated across the darkness. "My lady is a child still, I fear. A man takes his comfort where he can — with his wife, or with another willing lady. Once at court he will forget about you."

Lynette was so cold that her teeth chattered. "Why does it please you to — to hurt me?" she got out. "Because he took leave of me, and not you?"

"Who said he did not take leave

of me?" Johanna asked with a little laugh, and turned back into the rear chamber of the hall, closing the door behind her.

On half-frozen feet Lynette climbed back up the stairs and huddled in her bed, shuddering. Edgar had taken private leave of Johanna, though he would have gone without a word to her, his wife! And where had he spent the night?

She felt that her heart had died, that nothing mattered any more as she lay watching the first faint light of dawn grey the outlines of the window.

"My lady?" the maid Acha's voice came from the doorway.

"Yes," Lynette said listlessly. "Come in."

The child had come to make up the fire, bringing a pan of hot embers and some thin branches. She sat blowing on the fire until the branches caught, then added a log or two and went to bring Lynette some water.

Sitting on the edge of her bed,

Lynette shuddered and drew on her robe. She had found it in the chest, though it was not new. Perhaps it, too, had belonged to Edgar's mother.

"Don't look so sad," Acha said as she returned with a bowl and towel. "My lord will not be gone for ever."

"Do I look sad?" Lynette asked.

"Yes, all the time. Except yesterday, when you spoke to the people. Ulf said you looked proud then, because you were with Lord Edgar."

"Ulf seems to tell you a great deal," Lynette said, smiling despite the void inside her. "No — do not leave, Acha. Stay and help me dress. I need a maid."

Acha's brown eyes widened until they almost eclipsed her face. "Me, my lady? But I don't know how."

"Then I shall teach you."

To her surprise, Acha's head dropped and she pulled unhappily at her dark hair. "As you will, my lady."

"I thought it would please you," Lynette said. "You would attend me, and sleep in this chamber with me while my lord is absent."

"Yes, my lady, but — I could not be your serving maid and also the wife of Ulf, could I? Who would cook his food?"

Lynette stared at her. "Ulf's wife? Is this arranged?"

"Oh, yes, my lady! We are to wed come harvest time. My lord agreed, and my father and Ulf's father."

"But Acha — how old are you?"

The child screwed up her face, thinking. "I don't know. But I was born at harvest-time the year King Rufus came to the throne."

"King William," Lynette corrected. "They call him Rufus because he has a red face."

Acha giggled merrily "They say he is very fat, too, like a barrel of ale. Have you seen him?"

"Only once, and that from a distance." She remembered the knighting ceremony outside the walls of Lincoln. How long ago it seemed. "Well, Acha, I calculate that you will be thirteen come harvest. And Ulf?"

"A few years older. Oh, my lady, I do want to marry him! But if you say I must be your maid — "

"No," Lynette sighed. "I would not keep you from Ulf. You love him very much?"

"Oh, yes, my lady!"

A pang of envy surprised Lynette. How stupid of her to be jealous of the child's happiness. But she suspected that Acha and Ulf would have more joy of their marriage than she could hope for. Happy the girl who was allowed to follow her own heart.

"Then serve me until harvest-time," she said. "And stay now and help me. These lacings make my arms ache."

Dressed in a serviceable dark blue, Lynette made her way down to the great hall, where she found Johanna and Ned awaiting her arrival. The valley priest had come from the church to lead the daily ritual of morning prayers by the small crucifix in the centre of the hall and everyone involved in the household attended the brief service.

Sitting in Edgar's armed chair by the high table, Lynette found herself flanked by Johanna and Ned, with Ned's wife beside him. She had discovered that Ned was chief steward and would oversee work in the valley during Edgar's absence.

"When I have seen the bailiff and organised work for the day," he said, "I intend to ride round the manor, to see that all is in order. If you would care to come with me, my lady, I should be honoured."

"Thank you, Ned," Lynette replied, "but I think this morning I must stay at home and take note of household affairs. After dinner, perhaps — "

She was interrupted by Johanna, who delicately broke a piece of bread and tossed it to the dogs. "The household runs smoothly, my lady. It need not concern you."

"But it does concern me," Lynette

argued. "It is my duty to oversee the work of the great hall. It will be no different from what I am used to. Since my mother died I have kept house at Braxby."

Johanna sighed to herself. "Very well, my lady, but you may find the servants will not take kindly to a Norman's orders. I have run this household for two years. I can continue to do so. My lord said it would be best."

"Did he?" She baulked at the thought of going against Edgar's orders, but he had given her the impression that he expected her to take up her duties at once. "All the same, I shall come with you."

Trailing behind Johanna, she examined the lower storey of the keep, where arms were stored against an emergency. In the upper store-room, bolts of cloth for clothes, towels and such-like were stored with tanned hides, dried herbs and other goods needed by the household, though Johanna gave her no time to study the stores in detail.

There were hawks in the mews, cared for by a falconer; oxen in the sheds; hunting dogs in a pen; chickens and geese scratching in the courtyard. Lynette saw the stables, the store of salted meat from last winter's killing — which was low and must be carefully rationed until after harvest, when the present year's beasts would be slaughtered — the dairy where butter was being churned and curds separated from whey: every out-house held some activity. What disturbed her was the surliness of the peasants when she was used to smiling faces at Braxby, and it was not only at her that the bleak looks were flashed but at Johanna, whose sharp tongue needed little excuse to lash forth and scourge some poor soul.

In the kitchens the bevy of cooks, maids and scullions were busy chopping vegetables, baking bread, preparing fowl, roasting and boiling and stewing. Two great fires made the air thick. Johanna poked her nose into everything, criticising even the way one girl was slicing onions, so that the girl, nervous, cut her finger and brought forth more rage from Johanna.

As they came out into the cooler air of the courtyard, Lynette said, "I found at Braxby that the servants responded better to kindness, Mistress Johanna."

"Well, here we believe in keeping peasants in their place," Johanna replied. "They know they will not get the better of me. Treat them lightly and they will be off dallying, or poaching, or some other mischief."

"Is that Sir Edgar's philosophy?"

"Neither he nor Ned interferes in my affairs," Johanna said.

"But they are now my affairs," Lynette pointed out.

Johanna reddened, but her eyes flashed a warning. "I had thought to ease your way, not to interfere. But if you wish Sir Edgar to return to a house in turmoil then by all means have it your way. Be kind to them. They will repay you with insolence."

"Johanna — " Lynette hesitated. "It

would please me if we could be friends. Surely there is no need for us to be at odds."

"There is no need for me to be here at all," Johanna said crisply. "I have two manors of my own in Northumberland. I came here because Edgar, being a bachelor, had need of a woman to oversee his household when his mother died. It may interest you to know that he would have married me, but that would never have done."

"Indeed?" Lynette's face felt stiff. "Why not?"

"Why, because although he may be a thegn by the Saxon way of thinking, under the Normans he is nothing but a poor household knight. He has nothing outside this valley — no lands or possessions granted by his patron Prince Henry — nothing but his sword, armour and war-horse. My husband was a rich man. To have married Edgar would have been disparagement, would it not?"

"That is what they call it," Lynette

said. "Then you refused him?"

"I refused to marry him." The slight emphasis on the word 'marry' hinted at other kinds of union. "But as I said last evening, my lady, marriage is a business arrangement. Until I find another husband I am content to stay here and serve Edgar — in whatever way I can."

She turned away and walked lightly towards the great hall.

Oh, no. No! Lynette cried inside herself. It was not true! Edgar would not have married her and brought her here if Johanna had been his mistress. No man would be so indiscreet. But she was dismayed by the jealousy that boiled inside her.

As Lynette crossed the courtyard she saw Edgar's black hound, Frith, lying forlornly in a patch of sunlight, chin on paws and such a look of woe in his eyes that she wondered if the dog, too, were sad that Edgar had had to leave so soon. She called to him, patting her thigh, and the dog lumbered to his feet, padding towards her with head down and tail between his legs, a picture of abject misery.

"Poor Frith," she said softly, scratching behind the shaggy ear. "You love him, too. You and I are same, for neither of us can tell him clearly how we feel."

As if it understood, the dog lifted its great head and looked into her face, grateful for some attention.

Lynette called to the falconer, on his way from the butchery with strips of raw meat for the hawks. She begged a few morsels off him and offered them to Frith, who licked the food from her fingers.

"He's always like that when my lord's away," the falconer volunteered. "Mistress Johanna has no time for him, so he lies around just waiting for Sir Edgar."

"Then he and I shall wait together," Lynette said, and stole another piece of meat from his bucket, flicking a shy smile at the man. "Thank you, er — "

"Lucas, my lady." He seemed surprised that she had bothered to notice him and with a bow he went away whistling. Lynette had made a beginning in her conquest.

That afternoon she rode out astride her own grey mare in company with Ned. The dog Frith trotted at her heels, won over by lavish gifts of scraps at dinner. In the fields the crops already showed green in those fields which had been sown first, though there was still some ploughing and harrowing in progress, the oxen toiling down the long strips, and elsewhere weeds were being pulled.

Ned pointed out certain of the peasants, telling Lynette a little about them and the services they owed to Edgar in return for the land they tilled. Most of the farmsteads were hidden in the woods, small houses of wattle and daub roofed with heather from the moors, which also provided food in the shape of rabbits and birds caught by the trained hawks. Edgar enjoyed hawking, so Ned said.

When they reached the end of the valley, Lynette dismounted and led her horse in beneath the trees to the pool where the waterfall splashed down the flank of the moor. The pool was edged with great flat rocks where Lynette sat down and cupped her hand to take a drink. She wore her cloak because the wind still had an edge to it, though the sun was growing warmer as the year progressed towards summer.

"You were with my lord in Lincoln, were you not?" she asked as Ned sat down beside her taking off the floppy bonnet he wore, while Frith lay close by her feet.

"Aye, my lady," the steward replied. "By rights he ought to employ men-at-arms, but he'd have to be able to trust them to bring them here. So the men of the valley take turns at being his escort. Nobody knows this dale exists — not even the Conqueror when he prepared his great book could find us.

But sooner or later we'll have to admit where we are. Sir Edgar's waiting the right moment."

"Then you, and the others, were acting as his body-guard when — when — "

"When we carried you off?" Ned supplied with a grin. "We were, my lady. We were the only ones he could trust. That court's full of intrigue — spies everywhere. I'm always glad when my time's over and I can come home. If I've got a quarrel with a man I'd sooner stand up and have it out with him than go creeping in corners like they do at the court."

Lynette trailed a hand in the cold water, feeling it numb her flesh. "Is that the way it is with my lord and Sir Miles of Louth? Creeping in corners?"

"Not exactly," Ned replied, but it seemed to her that his eyes were suddenly guarded as he glanced away from her and squinted at the sky. "We'd best be on our way if you want to see the rest of the manor, my lady."

"Oh, please, Ned," Lynette begged.

"Tell me the truth. Why does my lord so hate Sir Miles? He spoke of their meeting in combat some day, and if he is to be injured, or — or worse — surely I have a right to know why? What has Sir Miles done to him?"

He sighed heavily, leaning on his knee as he stared at the grass beneath his feet. "You know my lord saved Prince Henry's life?"

"Yes, I — I heard the tale."

"It was a few years ago, after the thegn Wulfrith died and left Sir Edgar as his heir. Sir Edgar could see no real future for any of us in the dale unless we found some way of joining the outside world again, so he went off and offered himself to serve Prince Henry — the prince was born in England, you know. Anyway, comes the day when they had to ford the river. It rained hard that spring and the rivers were all full. The prince's horse floundered and threw him off and he would have drowned if Sir Edgar had not risked his own life to save him."

"I heard that he swims like a fish," Lynette said.

"Aye, he does. Learned in this very pool here. And that was a wonder, of course, when most men can't swim and those that do only manage a few strokes before they sink like stones. The prince called Sir Edgar his magician and had him trained for knighthood."

Lynette considered the pool. Near the edges it was not very deep, but in the centre it dropped away into darkness beneath the rippling surface. A shiver ran through her as she thought of anyone venturing into that deep water. No wonder Edgar had earned the name of 'wizard'.

"It does not explain what lies between him and Sir Miles," she said.

"No, my lady." Ned frowned to himself, his brow deeply furrowed as he spoke unwillingly "The prince and his brother the king saw a chance to settle some of their differences by setting Sir Edgar and Sir Miles against each other. It was to be a friendly fight — coronets on their lances, so neither could be killed — but Sir Edgar eventually unhorsed Sir Miles and by accident one point of the coronet lodged under Sir Miles's helm."

His finger stabbed across his cheek and Lynette remembered candlelight glowing on Miles's fair hair and showing up that scar. A strange quirk of apprehension twisted her stomach as Ned went on:

"That was what did it. Sir Miles has never forgiven him for spoiling his pretty face. He has dubbed Sir Edgar 'Prince Henry's Black Saxon', and other things that get whispered behind hands."

He got to his feet, gathering the reins of his mount, and added, "I'll tell you one more thing, my lady — Sir Edgar has to watch his back. He was asleep one night when someone came at him with a dagger."

"Ned, no!" Lynette gasped. She stood up, startling the dog. "If the king's champion has a quarrel with

Edgar he will settle it honourably, for all to see, not — not with a dagger in the night."

"And in the back," Ned said grimly.

"But was the man not caught and questioned?"

"He was killed, by some who heard the commotion and came running. It seems he was a minstrel lodging overnight in Prince Henry's hall."

"Then he could have been sent by anyone!" she exclaimed. "Many people must distrust a Saxon knight who is so close to the prince. Oh, Ned! — But it could not have been Sir Miles. He would not stoop to such foul murder."

"No, my lady," said Ned, but his voice dripped irony as he turned away.

They rode back down the valley in silence, Lynette trying to still her alarm at what Ned had told her. Edgar might be riding into terrible danger. For him to face Miles in open, honourable combat was risk enough, but when she thought of his having an enemy who dared not even show his face she was sick with fear for him.

As she returned to her bed-chamber with Frith at her heels, she heard Johanna's raised voice.

"How dare you, girl! Don't lie to me. You came to steal."

"I did not!" Acha sobbed. "I swear I did not! My lady has made me her serving maid."

"You?" Johanna screeched, and swung round as Lynette went in. "I have caught a thief for you — this girl was rummaging among your clothes."

"I was seeing if any wanted mending!" Acha cried.

To Lynette's horror, Johanna struck the child across the face, sending Acha reeling across the room to collapse against the end of the bed.

"Mistress Johanna!" Lynette gasped, and beside her Frith raised his hackles and growled softly.

Johanna stared from Lynette to the menacing dog, as if she could not believe her senses. "Quieten that beast!"

"I would like to know," Lynette said, "why you take it upon yourself to enter my bed-chamber and strike my maid. If anyone is out of place here it is you, Mistress Johanna. I told Acha to make herself useful where she could."

"A peasant?" Johanna exclaimed. "Look at her — she is not fit to sweep the floors, let alone serve a lady."

"Then who do you suggest I should choose? Perhaps you would care to undertake the duties yourself?"

It was clear from Johanna's outraged expression that she was insulted by the suggestion, though Lynette knew that women of high station did serve as ladies-in-waiting, especially if they were widowed, or before they wed.

"You go too far, my lady," Johanna said, violet eyes cold in her white face. "I shall return to my own manor as soon as possible."

"As you wish," Lynette replied. "I will ask Ned to supply you with an escort."

"No. My lord will supply me with an escort when he returns. At this time of year none can be spared from the fields. I shall be your guest until then — my lady."

She swept a deep, mocking curtsey and started only for the door to be stopped by a fresh growl from Frith, who clearly had no love for the pale haired widow. Swallowing a smile, Lynette drew the dog aside and Johanna passed in a swirl of skirts, slamming out of the room in a furious temper.

"I was not stealing!" Acha sniffed.

"I know you were not," Lynette replied. "Come, up with you. If you are to be my maid you must learn to behave like a lady. Before supper you must wash your face — with soap — and comb your hair. And see the laundry-woman. If the clothes I arrived in are dry, you may mend them and wear them. I shall see that more tunics are made for you, in due course."

Rather than being pleased, Acha

looked unhappy. "Ulf will think I am grown too grand for him, my lady."

"Nonsense! I shall find him a suitable post, too."

Acha goggled at her. "Would you, my lady? Oh — he would love to be allowed to help train the hawks — to be a falconer."

"Then I shall speak to Lucas and see if he needs an assistant. Say nothing to Ulf yet."

"Oh, no, my lady! Oh, thank you, my lady! Thank you!"

How easy it was to please her, Lynette thought fondly. But Acha and Ulf deserved to be rewarded for their loyalty to their new mistress. The valley would see that a Norman could be grateful.

As the days passed, Lynette's confidence increased. The sun grew warmer and so did the feelings of the people in the valley towards their new mistress. She took care to learn all their names and remember if one of them was sick. And with Ned's approval she installed Ulf as apprentice falconer.

She learned, too, the secret of the watchman's horn: two notes told of someone approaching the valley and a third note meant that the arrival was a friend — perhaps the pack-horses returning from market. A succession of high-pitched notes, if ever they were sounded, would mean an attack by armed men, though everyone hoped such a call would never come.

Proud of her achievements, Lynette hid the pain in her heart, though at night, while Acha snored gently on her pallet and Frith snoozed across the end. of the great bed, her thoughts often left the dale and strayed to Edgar. Where was he now? Had he encountered Miles? And how was Hugo, alone at Braxby? Many times her pillow was wet with tears, but when morning came she rose smiling to go about her duties, with Frith beside her.

The dog became a great source of comfort. He followed her everywhere, which was a wonder to the servants who had been used to seeing Frith moping in corners during Edgar's absences. He was always ready to defend her and at quiet times she would sit stroking his head and talking to him softly about Edgar — to Frith she could speak her heart, for he could never reveal her secret yearning for her lord.

It was Johanna who struck the note of discord in the growing harmony. Several times Lynette issued orders only to find that Johanna had countermanded them, until the servants became confused. They were afraid of Johanna's sharp tongue and the swift slap she was wont to administer when roused, while Lynette was more gentle with them; so it was Johanna who was obeyed. Lynette began to see her authority threatened and determined to bring an end to the trouble.

Speaking to Johanna only made matters worse — the young widow would listen, coldly polite and all "Yes, my lady," then go away and change something Lynette had ordered.

Impatiently, Lynette waited for the right moment. It came on a bright morning in late May, when a mist across the valley promised a fine day.

Lynette woke full of energy and when she had breakfasted she ordered a great clean-out of the hall. The floor was to be swept, the hangings removed and the cobwebs dusted away, then the whole place must have a fresh coat of whitewash, inside and out. Having seen the work begun Lynette went to the keep to check the stores, but half an hour later, when she returned to the hall, she found it almost empty. The floor had been swept, as it was every day, but nothing else had been done.

Annoyed, Lynette questioned a boy who informed her that Johanna had put a stop to the work.

"Fetch her to me," Lynette said grimly. "And fetch all the others, too. It is time they discovered who is mistress here."

She waited, pacing the hall with Frith trotting expectantly at her side, and slowly the house-servants began to creep back into the hall, whispering among themselves. Finally came Johanna, walking unhurriedly and proudly, a sympathetic smile on her face.

"My lady," she said sweetly, "I crave your pardon, but being a stranger here you would not know that the hangings have not been disturbed for years. By now some of them are old and delicate. To take them down and beat them would destroy them, and I do not think my lord would be pleased if he returned and found them gone. The pictures are part of the heritage of this valley. They tell the tale of how Wulfrith found the dale and Wulfnoth his son was killed while fighting with Hereward the Wake at — "

"I know," Lynette broke in. "But the spiders are thick behind them, to say nothing of dust and smoky grime. I like a clean house, Mistress Johanna. And — " she added as Johanna opened her mouth " — if my lord objects then I shall answer to him myself."

"But the hangings — "

"If they come to harm, we will make new ones. There must be artists in the valley who could copy the pictures. But we shall have the hall cleaned!"

"You are stubborn, my lady," Johanna muttered.

Glancing round at the servants who had heard most of this exchange, Lynette laid her hand on Johanna's arm. "I am most grateful to you for showing me my duties. You are an honoured guest, Mistress Johanna, but the responsibilities have been heavy. I relieve you of them, and if my lord is displeased his displeasure shall fall on me. From now on, spend your time pleasantly and leave the work to me."

Seeing the fury on Johanna's face, she spun away and clapped her hands. "Come! There is much to be done. I shall help you, if you will help me."

She was aware that most of the servants shared Johanna's fears about damage to the hangings, but she chivvied them along and hid her own disquiet. The hangings were very important to the dale people and if any harm came to them because of her they would never forgive her, but once set on the course she dared not back down in front of them all. She only prayed her decision would not prove to have been folly.

To the servants' surprise, their young mistress supervised every aspect of the work personally, watching as the hangings were taken down with great care and taken out to be shaken before being lowered into tubs of lye soap and gently paddled. She had men climb ladders to sweep the high corners and the rafters, and once took up a broom herself to demonstrate how the floor should be swept; then she went out to oversee the laying of the hangings over bushes to dry in the sun.

Unfortunately, Johanna had been right about the poor state of some of the linen and with dismay Lynette saw the holes in the worn material, and the faintness of the paintwork. Unless she could repair the damage there would be trouble from the people, and probably from Edgar, so as soon as the hangings were dry she set several of the women to darning.

For three days the work went on and gradually the hall was transformed. Where the walls had once been grey they shone white and Wulfrith's bronze helm was given an extra burnish by Lynette herself, so that it gleamed proudly on its hook. Now all that was needed was the return of the hangings.

Seeking Ned's advice on the matter, Lynette ordered paint to be mixed from the stores and several people set to work to restore the colours on the hangings, laying the work out on the floor of the great barn, where stocks of corn were running low and leaving ample space. Finally the hangings were replaced in the great hall and when the last one was hung a spontaneous cheer went up. With relief, Lynette knew she was well on the way to winning her battle for recognition.

Exhausted by the prolonged effort, she fell into bed on that warm May night and slept almost at once.

Frith's growling reached down into her dreams. She woke with a start as the dog sat up at the end of the bed, barking, and the flicker of the rush light showed her a figure by the door — a tall figure in a ragged cloak with a hood drawn down to conceal his face. In his hand a dagger-blade glinted faintly.

Lynette sat up, holding the blankets to cover her nakedness, staring in terror at the intruder. Where was Acha? Her pallet lay empty.

"Keep the dog quiet!" the man whispered in French. "I wish you no harm, my lady. But I must speak with you."

Lynette thought she recognised the voice, but she doubted her own ears. She spoke sharply to Frith and he subsided, though his growls continued and he watched the intruder alertly.

"Who are you, sir?" Lynette breathed.

"How dare you — "

"I dare not come any other way," he said, and threw back the hood to reveal his face. Lynette stared, shocked beyond speech. It could not be, and yet it was. The intruder was none other than Miles of Louth.

8

"MILES?" Lynette said faintly, wondering if she were still dreaming.

"Aye, Miles." His voice was rueful. "Such tricks are not to my liking, but it seemed the only way. God's blood, but he protects you poorly."

She tucked the blankets more firmly under her arms as he stepped closer. "I am in no danger here."

"No danger! How can you say that?"

The tone of his voice made Frith rise up, growling more fiercely, and Lynette called the dog, patting the bed beside her. Frith came to the place, lying on the blankets with his body heavy against her leg as he lay watchful. Knowing he was liable to attack Miles, Lynette caught the thick hair at the back of his neck and held the dog firmly.

"What do you want here?" she asked, her voice still hushed with horror. Instinct told her to call the guards, but though she no longer felt anything for Miles he was still a Norman knight and she knew the Saxons would cut him down if they discovered him in her bed-chamber.

Sheathing his dagger, he dropped to one knee and held out his hands to her, his face anguished in the flickering light. "My love, I know what he has done. He has lied to you and turned you against me, that black Saxon dog! He is not to be trusted, however sweetly he may have wooed you. I know the fault is not yours. Whatever he has done to you, I will forgive you. I love you still."

Lynette struggled to understand her own feelings. She ought to be glad to see Miles, for his presence promised escape from the valley, but instead she was shocked by his appearance in her bed-chamber and she wished he would not make avowals of love to her now that she was another man's wife.

Besides, she had no wish to leave the dale, not now.

"How did you come here?" she asked.

Miles gestured at his attire — a ragged tunic beneath the rough cloak. "I came as a beggar. Your steward let me sit at the back of the hall and get what scraps I could. I had to keep my face covered. There are those here who know me. My love, what has Edgar said to you? I know he would tell any lies to discredit me. But he is the black devil who carried you away from me. And he is worse, for he plots with Prince Henry to take the throne."

"No!" Lynette gasped.

"You doubt my word?" He rose to his full height, towering over the bed, and Lynette hung grimly onto Frith as the dog growled in warning. "My lady, has he turned your head so far — that you will believe his lies and not my truth?"

"What lies has he told me?" she asked desperately. "Miles, I am confused!

You come on me in the dead of night and — "

"And you fear me?" he demanded.

"No. No, I do not fear you, but I cannot think."

"Send the dog away," he suggested, "to prove that you trust me."

She hesitated, for she was not sure that she did trust Miles, not when she was naked and alone. "He will not leave me while you are here. Whatever you have to say, say it."

"Your father will be grieved by the change in you," Miles said.

"My father?" Forgetting her wariness, she grasped eagerly at the chance of news of home. "Oh, Miles, how is he? Tell me, have you seen him? All these weeks I have not even known if he still lived."

"He is well enough," he replied. "But he is anxious about you. We have both been anxious, fearing what that fiend had done to you."

"Fiend?" Did he mean Edgar? Strangely, the word did not apply to the man she knew.

"That villainous pagan!" Miles exclaimed, his gaze caressing the bare skin of her arms and shoulders. "When I think of him touching you I am near mad with jealousy. He is a devil, a defiler of women. And a traitor! Were it not for my promise to the king to hold my temper in check he would have died long ago. But the king believes Prince Henry's smiles and fair words."

"Miles, they are brothers!" Lynette protested.

"Aye, but there are dark plots afoot. I know it. And Sir Edgar is deep embroiled in them. Watch him, my love. Listen to his private words and remember them. Together, you and I will bring down this dog of a Saxon."

"Are you asking me to spy on him?" she asked incredulously. "Miles — there has been no breath of treason. And besides — " she felt it only right to tell him the truth " — I am his wife."

He stared at her blankly, searching

her face. "His wife? He forced you to — "

"He did not force me!" She spoke so earnestly that even to her own ears it sounded like truth. "I came willingly. It was wrong of me, I know, and I beg you to forgive me, but if anyone is to blame it is I and not Edgar. Why continue this feud? There are many women who would gladly take you for husband. Am I so important, with my one small manor?"

"You are of great importance to me!" he said passionately, pacing the room to the accompaniment of fresh growls from Frith. "This is hard to believe. When did you marry him? Where? Who were the witnesses? Did he cast a spell on you? Aye — that must be the answer — he has bewitched you!"

"Perhaps he has," Lynette replied with a sigh. "But not with spells or mystic potions. Forgive me, Miles, but please say to my father that I am well and happy. My lord treats me well. I want for nothing."

Miles stopped his pacing and threw out his arms. "I wish now that I had come armed, with a strong escort, but I had to spy out his defences first. I would take you away and undo this spell, but the valley is well-guarded. We could not get far, and to raise a hue and cry at this stage would only put both our lives in danger. You must stay here, for the time, and listen to what passes. The king will reward us well when the work is done."

"And if there is nothing to hear?"

"There will be! He works towards a Saxon uprising. He wormed his way into Prince Henry's affections and now he seeks to turn the prince against the king. When the land is torn by strife, then will the Saxons rise. Will you work for them, or will you stand with your own people?"

Lynette shook her head wildly. "I do not know! I cannot believe he is so treacherous. Miles, how did you discover it was Edgar who had taken me? How did you find this valley?"

"I have my spies," he said with a dismissive gesture. "I know what that Saxon dog had on his mind when he took you. He is trying to force me to issue a challenge. But never fear, my love, he shall not goad me into striking before I can reveal the true blackness of his soul. I shall choose my moment and when I have rid the land of this scheming husband of yours I shall come for you."

The hatred on his face when he spoke of Edgar was frightening to see. Lynette realised with horror that the next time she saw Miles it might mean that Edgar was dead. Her heart nearly stopped at the thought and she sent up a silent prayer: Dear heaven, guard him! Bring him home to me!

"Meanwhile," Miles went on, "your father grieves for you. Let me take something of yours to prove to him that you are alive and well."

"But what?" Lynette breathed. "I brought nothing with me save the clothes I had on, and those I have given to my maid."

He studied her, his eyes on the bright waterfall of hair that fell about her. "A lock of your hair will do. Few women have such hair. My love, I need some token. Your father fears you are slain."

"Then — very well. Lend me your dagger. But carefully, Miles, or I will not be able to hold the dog if he attacks."

Slowly, he removed the dagger from its sheath and, his eyes on the alert Frith, tossed it onto the bed.

"Stay, Frith," Lynette ordered, reaching for the dagger. She cut off a lock of her hair and stared for a moment at the red-gold curl lying on her palm. "This will have to do. But tell him you have seen me, Miles. Why should he doubt you?"

"An anxious father needs proof positive," Miles said, and stepped nearer to take the lock of hair and the dagger. As he did so he seized her hand and bent to kiss it fervently.

"Thank you, my love."

Disturbed, Lynette withdrew her hand and curled it in the blankets. She had no desire for Miles's kisses now she had experienced Edgar's lips on hers.

"Now I must leave you," Miles said. "But remember — watch the Saxon. Watch and listen. Here in his own lands he will unguard his tongue. You may hear the very heart of his plotting, especially if you are persuasive as a woman can be. He is only a man, and susceptible to a woman's charms. Farewell."

As the door closed behind him, Frith woofed softly to himself and settled down nose on paws while Lynette scratched his head, her eyes on the door. If she was not mistaken, Miles had suggested she might use her body to trick Edgar into talking freely. Was that the thought of a valiant knight, a future husband who professed to love her? She could hardly believe that she was fully awake and had actually seen

Miles — Miles the dauntless, champion of the king — disguised as a beggar and plotting to employ her as a spy against her own husband.

She lay down, shivering, as Frith climbed back to his accustomed place at the end of her bed. She wondered if her love for Edgar was, indeed, the result of a spell which he had cast on her. But Edgar was no wizard. That was a tale he liked to encourage, as he encouraged the legend of his being brought up among wolves. He was amused by the mystery that surrounded him.

And he was not a traitor, plotting to set Prince Henry on the throne to further the Saxon cause. Miles was wrong. Wrong! William Rufus himself had employed Saxon knights in his struggle with Normandy. The two peoples were beginning to work together and Edgar was trying to advance the union, not planning a rebellion.

Deeply disturbed by Miles's visit, she

hugged her pillow in misery, her heart crying out for Edgar. When would he come home? Oh, when?

She slept fitfully, waking at each slight sound in the fear that Miles had returned, so when the latch clicked she was awake at once. The rush-light had flickered its feeble last and the room lay in darkness, but as Lynette held her breath she heard Frith stir and woof, and Acha's voice whispered, "Hush, Frith."

"Acha?" Lynette said sharply.

The child gasped. "My lady?"

"If this continues," Lynette said as her heart resumed its usual steady pace, "I shall send Ulf back to his father's house and he shall not be a falconer."

"I'm sorry, my lady," Acha whispered.

Lynette closed her eyes against the tears that stung them. Thank God the child had not been there when Miles came! Instead she had been safe in Ulf's arms. Life was so simple for peasants — they loved where they chose and no one criticised them for it. Acha and Ulf were just two healthy young animals, innocent as the beasts in the forest.

She turned over, burying her head in the blankets to stifle her sobs. Edgar! Oh, Edgar, come home!

At breakfast the following morning she asked Ned what had become of the beggar who had craved alms and shelter the previous night.

"He left at first light," Ned said. "Did I do wrong, my lady? He was a pitiful sight — young, but crippled with wounds got in battle, and a face so hideous with sores he dare not reveal it. I was sorry for him."

"We must offer charity where we can," Lynette replied. "But another time, Ned, I would prefer to be warned when strangers come. I missed hearing the watchman's horn, and had it not been for Acha's gossip I would not have known we had a stranger among us."

"Your pardon, my lady," the steward said. "I would have told you, but you were tired and it did not seem important. One poor beggar can't harm us."

Little you know, Lynette thought, but she smiled and turned the conversation to work on the manor.

In the fields the lambs and calves grew apace.

Lynette rode out with Ned some afternoons to check the growth of the crop and other times she accompanied Lucas and Ulf to the moor with the hawks. Lucas had a merlin falcon suitable for a lady's wrist, but she refused to learn how to fly it for it caught larks and she preferred to hear the little birds sing rather than to eat them in a pie. Her tenderness amused the falconers, but they respected her for daring to hold views of her own.

May turned into June and still Edgar remained at the court. Several days' downpour of rain caused concern over flattened crops, but when the sun shone forth again the corn straightened and the fear was past.

During that time Johanna kept herself away from Lynette except at mealtimes. She said she and her personal maid were engaged on a tapestry and sometimes the two could be heard singing in the bed-chamber at the rear of the hall. A life of ease appeared to suit the young widow, though she seemed to Lynette to be like a contented cat which might at any moment unsheath its claws.

On Midsummer's Eve a great bonfire was built on the green where three oak trees spread their branches opposite the gate of the manor house. After supper, as the sun went down, everyone gathered on the green and Ned laid a torch to the fire. Soon flames and smoke curled up towards the darkling sky and through the dusk came the lights of other torches as all the people of the dale walked in procession to join the celebration.

With Frith beside her and Acha not far behind, Lynette walked across the drawbridge to watch as the fire flared brighter. Its flames would frighten away demons and witches that might harm the growing crop, and the smoke drove away diseases from the corn.

Someone had brought a pipe and struck up a tune, so that soon a ring of laughing, singing people danced round the fire.

"We're set fair for a good harvest this year," Ned said as the ale jugs went round. "Barring storms, we'll fill the barns to the rafters. You've brought us luck, my lady."

"Do you think so?" Lynette replied with a shy smile. "Oh, Ned, I hope the people believe that it is so. I love this dale."

"You love its lord," Ned said with a wink.

Dismay made Lynette draw back. Was she so transparent? Had she given herself away?

"Well, didn't you tell them all so, the day you arrived?" he reminded her. "They talk of it still."

"Oh — yes. Yes, of course." Her

heart fluttered in relief. She had forgotten that as far as the villagers were concerned she and Edgar were happily espoused.

One of the women brought her a mug of ale, offering it as though she expected to be refused. Lynette smiled, remarked that bonfires were thirsty work, and drank deep of the foaming brew, to the delight of all who saw.

"We'll make a Saxon of you yet," Ned said.

When the best blaze of the fire was over, the faggots were separated with a hay fork into two piles and the people began to run across the sparking ashes which remained between the fires. Red light licked across their faces as they ran, the women guarding their skirts. Some were timid and needed encouragement, but others ran boldly.

"My lady should go, too," a voice croaked, and Lynette recognised the old woman who had presented her with the cradle. "Purify yourself, my lady. Leave the past behind."

Some among the crowd would have silenced her, but she shrugged them off and stared challengingly at Lynette. "Are you afraid? Is a Norman afraid of a little fire?"

Lynette had watched this rite at Braxby often enough, but had never taken part. She glanced at Ned for help, but his expression said the choice was hers.

"Purify yourself!" the old woman cried again. "Cleanse yourself ready for your own harvest — a son for the dale!"

The words caused Lynette's heart to turn over, but maybe this was a chance to convince them all that she was one of them. She gathered up the fullness of her skirts, looking warily at the narrow path of dark ashes between the fires. The wind blew the flames this way and that.

As she hesitated, she was aware of gasps behind her and the crowd stirred, but before she could turn to see what was causing the disturbance someone grasped her arm, swinging her round. She felt herself swept up in strong arms as she looked into Edgar's dark face.

Instinctively, her arms went round his neck as he strode with her through the midst of the fires, to a shout of cheering.

"Edgar?" she said dazedly, unable to keep the joy out of her voice. "Oh — Edgar!"

He clasped her tightly to him, gazing down at her with such a light in his eyes that she was glad the firelight hid her blushes.

"A son for the dale," he murmured, long strides carrying them both through the ring of people to the road.

Lynette's happiness evaporated as she leaned her head on her arm, watching the fires and the shadowy people who called and laughed after them. That was all she meant to him — a mother for his heir.

She became aware that Frith was running alongside, barking angrily as if disturbed by the commotion of his master's arrival. Laughing, Edgar set Lynette on her feet and bent towards the dog, but Frith backed off, still barking.

"What's this?" Edgar said in surprise, straightening.

"He thinks you were attacking me," Lynette said in a small voice.

"He thinks — " Edgar began incredulously, and broke off to shout his laughter to the stars. "Great God, I have been away too long. This red-haired Norman witch has charmed my people — and my dog. My lady, what spell have you used?"

"If love is a spell then you may name me witch," she replied dully.

"Love?" His voice was soft as he drew her close to him. "Then will you cast that same spell on me, my lady?" Lynette turned her head away, bitter thoughts making her want to hurt him, to bring him out of this mood of dangerous good spirits. "On you it would be wasted. Bed me if you must. Get sons on me if you can. But do not ask for my love, too. I know well enough why you married me, and it was not for desire of my heart. You already have what you want, sir."

"So the war goes on," Edgar said, and she fancied there was regret in his voice as he released her and stepped back with a sigh. "I have ridden full gallop all day — for this."

He began to walk away, the spring gone from his step, and Lynette followed, with the dog beside her.

Torches sputtered in the courtyard where Edgar's companions were unsaddling their sweating horses, and out from the great hall came Johanna, dressed in her finest and glittering with jewels. She swept a curtsey as Edgar paused.

"You must be tired, my lord. I shall order food to be brought."

"No food," Edgar said shortly. "I am past hunger. Send up a jug of wine."

He strode on towards the keep and Lynette saw the faintest smile of satisfaction on Johanna's face. It sent a thrill of anger through her, for it had been her place to offer Edgar refreshment, not Johanna's.

When he reached the bed-chamber, Edgar threw off his sword and seated himself on the edge of the bed, his elbows on his knees as he stared at the floor. No fire blazed on that warm night, but the soft dance of rush-lights lit the room. Lynette, standing by the door with Frith at her feet, watched her lord and thought how weary he looked. It was strange when strength had flowed through him as he carried her through the fire.

A servant brought wine. Edgar drained the first cup and allowed Lynette to pour another, not looking at her.

"What news of your father?" he asked at length."

"He is — " Lynette began, but stopped herself. She had had no news save that which Miles had brought. Did Edgar know of the visit? "News of my father?" she said nervously.

"Aye." He glanced across at her, deep shadows beneath his eyes. "Godwin brought it, did he not?"

"Godwin?" She was bewildered. "I know no Godwin."

"I sent him off to Braxby that very day we arrived here," Edgar said, frowning. "I told him to bring news as soon as he could. Two months — you mean he has not returned?"

"If he has, he brought no word to me."

With a curse, Edgar pulled himself to his feet and brushed past her. She heard him in the courtyard shouting for Ned and a few minutes later he came back, his brow lined with bleak anger.

"Some misfortune must have overcome him," he said. "Yet Godwin is the most cunning of my men. God's teeth, if he has been taken — "

"Taken by whom?" Lynette asked, trembling with apprehension.

"By someone intent on interfering with my affairs," Edgar growled, and flung his cup at the fireplace so that wine spilled down the wall. "I must sleep. My thoughts are cloudy. Whose pallet is this?"

"My — my maid, young Acha. But she will sleep elsewhere tonight, knowing you have come home. My lord — if you wish to use your own bed — "

"I intend to," he said flatly. "And you may sleep where you please, my lady. I am too weary to care."

He threw himself face down on the bed, limbs sprawled in exhaustion. On such a warm night he would get little rest if he remained fully clothed, Lynette thought. But she baulked at the thought of offering to help him undress.

She bent and picked up a corner of the pallet, dragging it through the doorway into the adjoining room while Frith watched in puzzlement.

"Stay, Frith," Lynette breathed. "Stay and guard him," and she closed the door, leaning on it. She might dream sweet dreams of loving Edgar, but when he was there in person he only reminded her that he did not love her in return.

As dawn came over the hills, Lynette woke and swiftly threw on her clothes before Edgar could discover her; then she softly opened the door of the bed-chamber.

Frith lay on the floor, but roused himself as Lynette approached the bed where Edgar slept. Sweat soaked his hair and the pillow, for he was still fully dressed. He looked so vulnerable that she wanted to lie beside him and put her arms round him, waking him with kisses. But if he woke she would see the scorn in his eyes, or perhaps the desire unsoftened by love. Filled with sadness, she moved silently away, breathing, "Stay, Frith. Stay."

The household servants, hollow-eyed after their revels the previous night, had begun to stir when Lynette reached the courtyard. She caught Acha, on her way to take water to the bed-chamber, and instructed the girl to stay away from the keep while Edgar slept.

"Where is Sir Edgar?" Johanna asked as they met for breakfast.

"Sleeping," Lynette replied. "He was so tired I thought it best to let him rest."

"The men say they rode hard all day yesterday, taking food and drink in the saddle," Ned put in. "My lord was very anxious to be home."

"Then it is a great pity I must take him away so soon," Johanna said, studying a garnet ring on her finger. "I must be taking leave of you all and returning to my own manors."

"You expect Sir Edgar to escort you?" Lynette asked incredulously.

"I certainly would not trust my safety to anyone less than he," Johanna retorted. "Nor would he expect it. I regret that it will mean robbing you of his company again, but it should not take more than a week — unless he chooses to visit a while with me."

Irritated, Lynette turned to Ned.

"Tell me about the man Godwin. My lord said he was sent to Braxby to bring news and has not returned."

"Aye," Ned said with a frown. "I kept it from you, my lady, not wanting to worry you. Godwin must be dead, by some accident or — "

"Or he has been captured?" Lynette supplied.

"Why should anyone wish to capture him?"

"I don't know," the steward said, but his honest face was troubled.

"You do know, Ned," Lynette argued. "Tell me. My lord hinted at an enemy who might have taken Godwin. For what purpose?"

His frown deepened as he crumbled bread on the cloth. "We can't be sure, but we suspect he might have been captured by someone who was anxious to find the dale. If they were watching Braxby, they might have seen Godwin arrive and seized him as he left."

Lynette swallowed the alarm that had

got into her throat. "Who might, Ned? Who?"

"An enemy," was all Ned would say, but from his face Lynette read his meaning. He and Edgar suspected that Miles was responsible for Godwin's disappearance.

9

EVEN so early in the morning the day was hot as Lynette carried bread and wine up to the bed-chamber. She heard Edgar talking softly and found him sitting on the edge of the bed, ruffling Frith's ears as the dog sat in front of him.

"I thought you would be hungry when you woke, my lord," Lynette said, keeping her eyes lowered as she placed the platter and the goblet on one of the chests.

"I am flattered that you serve me yourself," Edgar replied. "Frith tells me that you and he have become good friends in my absence."

Despite the jesting words, he regarded her without expression. In another mood she might have laughed, but too many worries pressed on her.

"My lord — I have been speaking

with Ned about your man Godwin. Could it not be that he was overcome by wolves, or met with some other misfortune?"

"Aye, it could. We have no way of knowing."

Lynette bit her lip, but the words came bursting forth — "Then why do you think that Miles of Louth had a hand in it? Oh — no one has said so, but it lies behind your words. Every time some ill befalls you, you blame Miles for it."

"Not without good reason," Edgar said, his eyes watchful.

"But why do you think he keeps a watch on Braxby? Does he know how anxious you will be to acquire your rights in that manor? Is that it?"

A line appeared between his brows as he frowned. "My lady? What do you mean? Acquire rights — I?"

"Well, of course you will!" she said furiously. "When my father dies, that land will be mine — and therefore yours, since you are my husband. That is the only reason you married me — to regain the lands your ancestors lost to the Conqueror."

For a moment Edgar looked as though he did not understand her, then he stood up, glowering. "Who told you that?"

"Johanna did! Do not tell me it is untrue, for I will not believe you. Your grandfather Wulfrith was lord of Braxby, but was driven out — "

"Aye, that he was," Edgar said roughly. "From Braxby and all the lands around it. But I had long given up hope of regaining it."

"Until you met me! You have often sworn to win back those lands, have you not?"

"I may have done, but — My lady, I swear to you, when I wed you, Braxby was the last thing on my mind."

"But — " she faltered, seeing that he was telling the truth. "Johanna said — "

"Johanna was making mischief. What other lies has she poured in your ear?

God's teeth, that woman shall go home at once! Too long I have put up with her."

"She said that you — that you would have married her," Lynette said, her voice shaking.

"I'd as soon bed with a viper! I have given her a home because her step-sons — my cousins — turned her out because of her mischief-making. She had a choice between this valley or a nunnery."

"But she has manors of her own!"

Edgar laughed sharply. "Aye, manors near the coast where the weather is fierce. They bring in a goodly crop of fish, but the wind and rain make life unpleasant most of the year. Johanna fears for her soft complexion. But she shall go home, all the same."

Joy filled Lynette, but she allowed only a faint smile to curve her lips. "She is of the same mind, my lord. She wishes to leave today — with yourself as escort."

"Does she indeed? She asks too

much. I would not leave the dale so soon. There is work to be done."

Her spirits drooped again, though she chided herself for it. Had she really thought he might stay on her account?

"You will find everything in order," she said. "Ned is a faithful steward."

"And you a good housekeeper?"

"I have done my best. Maybe that is why you married me — to be rid of Johanna."

"Not so."

She spread her hands helplessly. "Then why, my lord? If not for Braxby — "

A shutter seemed to drop across his face, hiding all his thoughts. "Is it more pretty speeches you want?"

"No! I know well enough that you have no love for me. It was not love that impelled you to order your men to ambush us, nor love that made you wed me where no eyes could see."

"I told you — it was for your protection."

Sighing, she let her hands fall to her sides as she turned towards the door. "Very well, my lord. Do not be honest with me. I should have learned by now that such questions receive only devious answers."

"If I say it was to protect you from Miles of Louth — " Edgar began.

Lynette swung round. "How so? Miles was my betrothed. He loves me. He would not harm me."

"It was he who plotted to abduct you — and hold you to ransom."

She could not accept the enormity of what he was saying. "What?! But my father is a poor man! And Miles — How can you expect me to believe such things, sir? Miles had no need to hold me for ransom. He had only to wed me and — "

"He had no wish to wed you!" Edgar interrupted with a fierce gesture of his arm. "He has his eyes on a richer prize — a wealthy heiress in Normandy."

Lynette stared at him, blood roaring in her ears and her eyes stinging with tears. "That cannot be true! Oh, he said you would lie and I did not listen. I would not believe such things of you. But perhaps it's all true — perhaps you are a traitor, too!"

Blinded by hot tears, she felt him grab her and force her against the wall, his hands clamped round her shoulders. "Who said that?" he demanded. "Who?"

"Miles did. Miles did! Miles was here — see how safe your precious dale is! He came disguised as a beggar and Ned let him sit in the hall, and at night he crept up here and spoke to me."

"And you let him go free?" His eyes blazed into hers, mesmerising her. "You did not call for help? God's blood, he might have killed you!"

The words were almost drowned by Frith's savage barking. Startled by the dog's anger, Edgar released Lynette and stepped back. She bent to hold the dog, flinging back her head to stare at Edgar with tears glistening on her face.

"There is your answer, my lord. If Miles had tried to harm me, Frith would have torn out his throat. But Miles offered me no violence. He — he asked me to spy on you, to learn if you were plotting with Prince Henry against the king."

"Well, well," Edgar said, his voice deep with disgust. "You have done admirably, my lady treacherous. My people love and trust you — and now you would turn spy."

She stood up, her hands clenched. "If I had intended to spy, I would not have told you about it, sir!"

"Then why did you not call the guards to detain him?" he demanded.

"I had no wish to see his blood spilt on my account."

"No, of course not," he said bitterly. "You are very tender where his safety is concerned. How long was he here?"

"He arrived about suppertime, and was gone by — "

"I mean here, in this room!"

"Why — not long. But he did not

menace me, whatever you may think. Miles would not harm a helpless woman."

Edgar's gaze swept over her, suddenly alight with cold fire. "Then what did he do to you, my lady? God's eyes, was it a tender reunion, here in my own bed-chamber?"

"Edgar!" The implication in his tone shocked and wounded her. "How dare you — "

"How dare I?" he roared, and as Frith began to bark he flung open the door, ordering the dog out. "Go, Frith! Go!"

Frith hesitated, looking from his master to his mistress, then obeying the one he had loved longest he padded out and Edgar closed the door. Frightened by the black fury in her husband's face, Lynette backed away.

"Now, my lady faithless," he said in an undertone. "Perhaps I should remind you that you are my wife. Will you continue to deny me the favours you give so freely to other men?"

Trembling, Lynette sank to her knees, praying that he would not take her in anger, for surely that would destroy the love she had for him. "My lord, I swear, by all that is holy that I have never known a man."

"Aye," Edgar growled, his lip curling. "But then we know how great a talent you have for play-acting. You quiver like a virgin now. Did you quiver under Miles's hands?"

"Miles has not touched me!" Lynette cried. "Oh, why will you not believe me? No arms but yours have held me. No lips but yours have kissed my mouth."

Edgar's laugh was frosted by disbelief. "What, never? You go too far, my lady. Stand up and cease this display. I prefer it when you fight with me. Or would you even sink your pride for his sake — to blind me to the truth?"

One stride brought him to her side and he jerked her roughly to her feet, his hands tight around her arms. He held her there, imprisoned, while he dropped his mouth to hers and bent her like a bow until she overbalanced and fell across the bed, the weight of his body holding her there. His hands grasped the neck of her tunic and tore it from her, exposing the curves of milk-white breasts.

"Great God," he whispered. "You are beautiful. Swear to me Miles has not done this, nor this."

His hands made her skin feel alight where he touched it and Lynette lay helpless, watching his dark face work. Her arms lifted without her willing it and locked about his neck, drawing his mouth down to hers while her body surged with longings she had never known before. But in her mind Miles's voice sounded, saying, 'He is only a man, and susceptible to a woman's charms.' Yes, Edgar would take her because red blood coursed through his veins, and because he hated Miles, not because he loved her.

She braced herself to face the ordeal

which must come, her soul torn in two between her love for him and her despair. But Edgar suddenly wrenched away and stood staring down at her, the breath ragged in his lungs, his fists clenched.

"No!" he said hoarsely. "If there is to be an heir for the dale, let me not wonder who his father is!"

"Oh, sir!" Lynette breathed through, her tears. "I do not deserve such insults. I swear — "

"Time will prove you guilty or innocent," Edgar replied, his mouth twisting. "If you are with child — "

"I am not! I am not! I could not be!"

"Then if you are not," he said fiercely, "if you have told me the truth, then I shall do as I had planned and send you back to your father. You shall see whether I wed you for Braxby or not, my lady. Soon Miles will be rich enough to discard his hopes of your father's treasure and — "

"Treasure?" she got out.

" — and then you may go home," Edgar continued as if she had not spoken. "The marriage will be easily declared void, since there were no witnesses and you were unwilling. I will return you to your father as I found you — a maid undefiled."

He strode from the room without even a backward glance.

With a thudding head, Lynette drew her torn tunic to cover her and lay shivering despite the heat of the day. If Edgar planned to return her to her father, then what purpose had any of it served? She foresaw her future — a lonely one, away from all she had come to love so well. No Ned, no Acha and Ulf, no Frith, and worst of all no Edgar. Oh, he could not send her away!

She called for Acha to bring water and towels. The child came, questions in her eyes when she saw her mistress's torn clothing.

"Where is my lord?" Lynette asked.

"Gone down the valley," Acha

replied. "He's taken Frith with him. He said something to Lady Johanna about taking a swim, though if I were you, my lady, I'd stop him going near that pool. He'll drown himself if he's not careful.

"Sir Edgar knows what he is doing," Lynette said.

"But nobody else ever goes near that place! A goblin lives there!"

Lynette sighed to herself, guessing that the tale had been invented to keep children from straying to the pool at the risk of drowning. "My lord can deal with goblins. Hurry, Acha, get out some fresh clothes for me."

For her own sake she resolved to look her best, to hold her head up and pretend not to care that she was a mere pawn in something she did not understand. Ever since Miles had come to the dale she had been prey to uneasy thoughts about his intentions, and now Edgar had added fresh puzzles.

Had Miles waylaid the man Godwin and forced him to reveal the way to the valley? Had Miles thought to ransom her? But why? The mention of treasure was nonsense. As usual, Edgar had failed to explain anything fully, which was a trick of his. She could not understand why he did it.

Unless — the thought came painful — unless he had grown so tired of her disbelief that he no longer cared to explain anything. So many times pride had made her accuse him of untruth when instinct had told her she could trust him. Oh, why had she not listened to her heart before it was too late? Now he was so tired of her that he denied his own desire in order to leave the marriage unconsummated so that he could be free of her entirely.

When the horn blew to announce the hour for dinner, Lynette went down to the great hall expecting Edgar to be there before her, but he was absent. The household waited and the butler chafed by the screens, unable to begin serving until his lord arrived.

Either side of the carven armed chair

at the high table, Lynette and Johanna stood exchanging idle politenesses, though Lynette's mind kept straying to talk of goblins and drowning. She wished Edgar would come. She needed to talk with him, to ask his forgiveness and beg him to tell her what lay behind his strange words about Miles.

"Sir Edgar enjoys his pool on hot days," Johanna remarked "'Tis a strange habit, this swimming. But no doubt he thought to refresh himself before beginning our journey."

The blood rushed from Lynette's head, leaving her pale. "He said his duties would not allow him to leave the valley."

"Then he must have changed his mind, my lady," Johanna said with a sweet smile. "Why, just before he rode out this morning he assured me he would be riding with me. We shall set out after dinner, to make use of the long daylight."

Dismayed, Lynette was about to argue when a bustle at the back of the hall announced the arrival of Edgar himself. He strode in, wearing a clean black tunic edged with silver thread, his hair still wet from the pool. The cold water seemed to have invigorated him, though his smile was impersonal as he apologised for keeping them waiting.

Halfway through the first course, when he had taken the edge off his hunger, Lynette saw him notice the cleanness of the hangings. She held her breath as his gaze travelled round the newly-bright pictures adorning the drapes.

"We thought you would be pleased to come home to a clean house," Johanna said before Lynette could open her mouth. "We took great care of the linens, my lord. As you can see, they came to no harm. A little mending and a touch of fresh paint soon restored them."

"It looks well," Edgar said. "We should have done it before."

"I wanted to leave the house in good

order for you, my lord," Johanna said demurely.

Gritting her teeth, Lynette went on with her meal, though it tasted like chaff. She could hardly call Johanna a liar, not in public, but it irked her to have the widow take all the credit.

"I understand that Mistress Johanna plans to begin her journey this afternoon," she remarked.

Edgar glanced at her sidelong. "I thought I might ride at least part of the way, since I am not needed here."

The jibe found its mark and she was about to protest when he went on, "Ned appears to have everything well in hand, and the house is running with more smoothness than I have ever seen. There is an air of contentment that I missed before."

"I only hope that a mere Norman may run your house so efficiently," Lynette said stiffly, angry blood pounding at her temples. "In fact, my lord, I wonder if we can really do without Mistress Johanna! Perhaps you should ask her to stay!"

The words were torn from her as she wrenched herself to her feet and fled through the curtains, too hurt and angry to care what impression she had given to the rest of the household.

She ran up the stairs and gained the bed-chamber, where she paced restlessly, angry with the whole world, including herself. Edgar had promised he would not leave so soon, but no doubt Johanna had smiled and pleaded, wheedling him into agreeing to her demands. Perhaps Lynette should have smiled and pleaded, but it was always her temper that led the way, especially where Edgar was concerned. How could she be devious and sweetly sly when the very sight of him made every nerve in her body tremble? Artfulness had never been part of her nature as it was with some women, and with Edgar she was all fire or ice, never lukewarm.

She wandered about the bed-chamber and the sitting-room, hoping that Edgar might come; then she would tell him how Johanna had misled him. She would beg him not to go.

After a while, hearing a commotion in the courtyard, she looked from the window and saw the horses prepared for the journey, the outriders mounting up in their chain-mail jerkins. Edgar's black stallion was led out, and smaller palfreys for Johanna and her personal maid. The packhorses were laden with the widow's belongings.

Bitter despair made Lynette decide to stay in the keep and let Edgar depart without a word if he so wished, but when she saw him emerge from the hall with Ned she could not restrain her longing to be near him. Holding herself erect and proud, she hurried down the stairs, collected herself, and trod slowly across the courtyard.

"You have done well," Edgar was saying to Ned; "Ah — my lady, you too have played a part in this. The people of the dale are no longer so suspicious of Normans. It is time we revealed our presence to the king. The future lies under Norman rule. We may as well fight with them as against them."

Perplexed by his pleasant manner, she was lost for words until she remembered their pact to present a united front to his people.

"It will make life easier if we are not forced to hide like outlaws," Ned said. "I think you are right, my lord. The time has come."

Edgar glanced towards the hall as Johanna and her maid appeared. "The time has indeed come," he said under his breath, and took Lynette's hand. "My lady, I beg you continue your good work."

She caught her breath, seeing that he had not been misled by Johanna's lies.

"I knew your kindness lay behind the new feeling in the manor," Edgar said. "The servants have been restive under Johanna, and the house let go. I thank you, my lady." The black eyes held hers as he lifted her hand to his lips and gently kissed it. "I only regret your time here must be so short," he added so that only she could hear, and abruptly turned away to supervise the last details of the journey to the coast.

With so many people about she could not say the words she wished to say. She bade farewell to Johanna, irritated by the smugness in the widow's violet eyes; then she was obliged to stand by while the party mounted up and, with a final salute, Edgar rode out — again. Would he never stay in the valley two days together and give her time to talk to him?

"Best not stay out in the heat too long, my lady," Ned said as the last of the little cavalcade trotted over the drawbridge. "You should take care of yourself."

Puzzled, she watched his back as he walked away, then a bubble of laughter that was half sob broke from her. Her outburst in the great hall had caused speculation, as she had feared, though she had not suspected just what conclusion the servants would draw.

With Johanna gone and the corn growing full, the mood in the valley was high. Even Lynette began to share the sense of optimism, for when Edgar returned he would surely give her time to talk — to plead, if necessary. Pride would no longer stand in her way. She loved him and she had begun to suspect that he loved her, too, for she now believed that he had brought her here for protection and married her to keep her safe. Would he have done that if he had not cared for her, just a little?

She knew now that her constant rebuffs must have wounded him. Perhaps he was serious about sending her back to her father. But such thoughts were too painful to endure. She kept her hopes high, only living for the day when Edgar would return. Johanna had said the journey would take a week, there and back.

A week passed. Lynette listened eagerly for the sound of the watch-horn, but each time it sounded its reassuring three notes it heralded only the return of the traders from market, or a band coming home after gathering firewood in the forest. Lynette's jealousy made her begin to wonder if her husband had decided to stay with Johanna for a while. If that was the way of it then she had only herself to blame.

"My lady!" Ned came hurrying across the courtyard as Lynette examined the well one day. "My lady, a message has come. My lord left word with a trader — a friend of ours — at the market."

He shifted uneasily, twisting his bonnet in his hands.

"What did the message say?" Lynette asked.

"Sir Edgar — I'm sorry, my lady, but Sir Edgar has decided to go straight on to the court. The prince must need him."

Her face told nothing of the anguish inside her. "Thank you, Ned."

"Is there something wrong between you?" Ned asked. "Oh — I know it's not my place to enquire, but — he loves you, my lady. I know he does. He wouldn't stay away if — "

"If the prince has need of him, he must be with the prince," Lynette said sadly. "A wife comes a poor second to a knight's duty, Ned."

"Aye, my lady." He looked at her unhappily, as if he wanted to say more, but instead he bowed and excused himself.

Lynette stood quite still, drained of any desire to move. A great weight seemed to sit on her breast. Edgar was deliberately staying away from her because she had hurt him too often. Probably by the time he returned Miles's plans — whatever they were — would be fulfilled and she would be sent home, discarded.

Wulfrith's Dale lay contentedly beneath the July sun, but its mistress languished in depression, longing for her lord and knowing she had lost all chance of begging his forgiveness. But since she could not share her thoughts with anyone the servants formed their own opinion, sending her sly looks and winking at each other knowingly.

"I am not with child!" Lynette was driven to shout at Acha after a few days of unusual attentiveness on the maid's part. "Will you tell them so and put an end to this whispering behind hands? The dale will have to wait for its precious heir."

"Yes, my lady," Acha replied, but she looked thoughtful. Lynette's recent moods puzzled her, for if the mistress was not with child what could be causing her to look so heavy-eyed?

"Acha," Lynette said with a sigh. "Forgive me. I am weary — weary of my lord's absence. Would you be happy if Ulf were parted from you for weeks and weeks, with no end to it in sight?"

"No, my lady. I hate it when he has to go with Sir Edgar. But Ned says the men of the dale may stick to their fields from now on. Sir Edgar is going to hire men-at-arms to attend him now."

"Indeed?" She shook her head wearily. She was always the last to be told these things.

"It's strange," Acha said, twining an end of hair round her finger. "My lord doesn't usually stay away so long. Anyway, I expect he'll be home for harvest. He enjoys harvest. There's a great feast — and this year I'm to cut the last sheath and bring it home to the barn, all done with ribbons, because as soon as harvest is over Ulf and I — "

Her chatter trailed off and they both looked in disbelief at the window as the clear call of the watch-horn streamed across the valley, high notes blown fast in the alarm signal.

Acha clutched at Lynette, her eyes wide with fright. "Oh, my lady! An attack!"

Whirling to the door, Lynette ran down the steps as all the men of the household made for the keep to fetch weapons from the store. Ned was among them, calling orders, and Lynette saw other people running towards the gate from the fields. In the confusion she was brushed aside.

Never before had that alarm call sounded. Lynette shared the fears of her people, but her own fears had shape and form. Was it Miles, come to take his revenge after weeks of silence?

"Better get inside the hall," Ned said, appearing with sword and shield, a metalled jerkin flung on over his tunic. "Get all the women inside, my lady."

Thankful for something to do, she organised the women, making them go inside the hall. From there they could easily get to the safety of the keep should the palisade be breached.

"You, too, my lady!" Ned shouted as she waited by the door.

"No, Ned," she replied firmly. "This may be the trouble your people feared I would bring. If it is, I shall go myself to meet it."

"But my lady — " he protested.

Ignoring him, Lynette made her way

through the jostle of armed men bearing swords, crude lances and cudgels. She walked to the gate and saw that some of the peasants — mostly women and children come from their homesteads — were still running down the valley, frantically seeking the shelter of the manor.

"We must close the gate!" Ned cried.

"No! Leave it open. I shall speak with these invaders myself and ask their desires. It may be only me they want."

"And they shan't have you!" Ned said stoutly. "Not while I'm alive to prevent it. We didn't play brigand and fight off Sir Miles's bully-boys just to hand you over to them now. My lady, let me close the gate!"

There was no time to wonder what on earth he meant for the sound of hoofbeats could be heard, approaching at a steady pace. Through the trees appeared a small company of men-at-arms with two riders at their head. Neither of the two looked to be dressed for battle.

"Is it Sir Miles?" Ned asked. "There aren't many of them if — "

Lynette's gasp cut him off. She had just recognised the two figures leading the company, though for a moment she did not believe her eyes.

"It is my father!" she exclaimed. "My father and — and Ralf! Oh, Ned! Tell the men to put down their weapons. This is no attack force. It is my father!"

Joy lent wings to her feet as she sped across the drawbridge, but her steps began to slow as she realised what this surprising arrival meant — her father had come to take her home. She would probably never see Edgar again.

10

STANDING by the window of the small sitting room in the keep, Lynette watched as Ralf and her father disposed of the food and drink she had ordered for them. She was delighted to see them — of course she was, despite the heaviness of her heart. Her gaze lingered lovingly on the silver hairs gleaming on her father's head, and on Ralf's sturdy shoulders and rough-cut hair. How many times she had longed to see them again. But not like this. Oh, not like this!

At last Hugo sighed with satisfaction and set his goblet on the floor beside him. "You live well, my love. I heard Sir Edgar had a fine manor, but I did not expect anything like this. Private rooms!"

"Yes," Lynette said, only too aware of how much she loved the keep and the whole valley now that she must leave it. "I want for nothing — as Miles must have told you."

"Miles?" Hugo's face darkened. "That villain has told me nothing. If he had shown his face at Braxby, Sir Edgar's men would have cut him down. But I know he came to see you. I have proof here."

Reaching inside his tunic, he brought out the lock of hair she had herself cut with Miles's dagger. Lynette sank to the floor, taking the soft strands in her hand.

"But if you have not seen him — " she began with a puzzled frown. "Father, I do not understand! Was it all lies — everything he said?"

"Every word, if I mistake him not. God forgive me for ever wishing to see you wed a man like Miles of Louth."

"I tried to tell you, mistress — my lady," Ralf put in. "At the Abbey in Lincoln I heard things about him, but I feared you might say it was idle gossip, like the rest."

Lynette stared in bewilderment from Ralf's freckled face to her father's grave countenance. "Will you please tell me the truth?" she cried. "Edgar has told me nothing, save a few hints."

"Aye." Hugo's eyes glowed sternly. "He told us you would not believe him."

"He told you? Edgar told you? When?"

"A few days ago. But let us begin from the beginning. Ralf, this is your part of the tale."

Quaffing the last of his ale, Ralf wiped his mouth on his sleeve and leaned on his knees, his face full of excitement. "It was a fine thing to see. Sir Edgar cut down the leader of those brigands and his men dealt with the rest. I laid one flat with my cudgel." His arm flailed the air in demonstration, but Lynette was further puzzled.

"You are not being clear, Ralf. It was Sir Edgar's men who attacked us."

"No, indeed, my lady! Didn't you see?"

"I saw nothing! My cloak was over my head. Men came from the woods — "

"Aye, Sir Miles's men, in disguise!" Ralf told her. "I didn't know it then, of course. Sir Edgar told me later. They'd have killed him if his men hadn't come when they did."

Hugo lifted a hand for silence, laying his other arm across Lynette's shoulders. "It really begins with your grandmother, my love. When she visited us at Braxby she had doubts that Sir Miles, having grown so powerful, would wish to marry so poor an heiress. So I told her about the money I had saved for you."

"Money?" Lynette queried. "I knew nothing of — "

"No, I had kept it secret, as a surprise gift for you. Your mother had set a sum aside for you and I have added to it over the years. There must be near a thousand merks in the chest now. It is buried, in a place only I know. But I was wrong to tell your grandmother about it. She wrote to Miles and told him about this treasure, thinking to bring him hurrying to make you his bride. He came hurrying, right enough, but it was not marriage he had on his mind."

"He wanted the treasure? Then — is it true that he has betrothed himself to someone else?"

"He has. But the girl is only twelve years old and since he must wait for her to grow he decided to get your treasure to settle some heavy debts he owes. He must have been surprised to see you in Lincoln, but it gave him an opportunity to form his plan. He went straightway to his soldiers and arranged to have you abducted, to force me to hand over the treasure."

"How do you know this?" Lynette asked.

"Sir Edgar discovered it. When he met you, he knew of Miles's betrothal to the girl in Normandy. He was astounded to hear you say you were betrothed to Miles, and the mention of Braxby made him determine to find out what was afoot. He learned of some villainy plotted against you and against Braxby, so he came after you, to give you his protection, and he had his men follow in secret, should they be needed. They were. Miles's men came out at you and — "

"And we made them jump!" Ralf laughed. "You should have seen them run. But I was knocked on the head. When I came to it was dark and everyone had gone. Then Sir Edgar found me and told me the right of it. He sent me home to warn your father of Sir Miles's plot."

"He feared," Hugo said, "that in his frustration Miles might attack the manor. That is why he had you taken far away, out of danger. Then he hired men-at-arms to guard Braxby. They have stayed with us ever since, keeping watch for us. A short while later, a man named Godwin came to tell us you were safe and to bring back news for you, but I hear he did not return."

"Edgar thinks Miles has got him," Lynette said dully, feeling more mortified with every word.

"He may be right," Hugo replied. "It must have been Godwin who gave Sir Miles directions to find the valley. How else could he have come here? That bastard! Did he cut off your hair while you slept?"

Miserably, Lynette leaned on his shoulder. "I gave it to him freely. He said it was a token for you — to prove that I was alive. But if he did not give it to you how did you come by it?"

"Ah, that was another part of his plot." His voice rang with disgust. "Of course he could not come personally. No, he could not be seen to be involved. Instead he sent one of his men to Braxby. A message came for me — I was to meet with someone in the woods if I wished to hear news of you. Ralf came with me and this — this dissembler pretended to be a brigand. He said he had you captive — the lock of hair was supposed to be proof. He said he would return you if I gave him the treasure chest, but I sent him packing. I knew Sir Edgar would have sent word if aught had happened to you. 'Tell Sir Miles to bring me my daughter alive and well and he may have all I possess,' I told him. 'But unless I see her with my own eyes not a penny will he get from me.' The man went off, and that was the last we heard of it. Sir Miles must have been shamed into ceasing his attempts at thievery, if he has any shame. The man is a brute and a coward. He prefers to slaughter women and children rather than face a full-armed knight in equal combat."

"But he is the king's champion!" Lynette exclaimed.

"Aye, my love," Hugo said, stroking her head. "But even kings are not all chivalrous. William Rufus is a surly-tempered man. Should anyone cross him, he sends Sir Miles and his cut-throats to punish them."

Ralf leaned forward, adding eagerly, "That's what I heard at the Abbey. That's why I was so worried, but I never got a chance to tell you."

"The fault is not entirely with Miles," Hugo said. "He has to do as the king commands. That much I could forgive him. But to dishonour his betrothal vows and then to use force to extract money from me — that is unforgivable. Thank God for Sir Edgar is all I can say."

Lynette stood up, restlessly pacing the room. "Why did he not tell me himself? Father — if he had told me the truth from the beginning — "

"Would you have believed him?" Hugo interrupted. "You were convinced he had abducted you for some evil design of his own. Would you have listened to this tale of perfidy on the part of a man you regarded as a knight without stain?"

A heavy sigh escaped her. "No.

Perhaps not then. But later — "

"Sir Edgar said that you spoke of Sir Miles as if he were one of God's angels. You had a dream of him and you were not ready to let that dream go. Sir Edgar waited, hoping you would learn for yourself which one was the honourable knight. I told him he should have been truthful with you, but he had a dream of his own by then — he dreamed you might learn to trust him."

"But I do!" She spread her hands helplessly. "Of course I do."

"Have you told him so?"

Wearily, she shook her head. "How can I? He will never allow me close enough. And if he cares for me he takes pains not to show it. If only he had made me listen! And now it is too late. He has sent you to take me home, has he not?"

"That is what he said." Hugo rose from his stool and laid his hands on Lynette's shoulders, making her look at him. "He wished you to know the

296

truth and he thought you would believe it if I told you the tale. He gave us instructions on how to find this place, and he said we should come and escort you home."

"I see," she sighed.

"He wants no reward, no show of gratitude," her father told her. "I offered him the thousand merks, but he refused it. He said that although you were truly married he had not consummated the union and since the ceremony was unwitnessed — "

He left the rest unspoken, but it was plain enough. Such a marriage could be easily ended. Lynette looked into her father's kindly eyes and was reminded of the priest Machel telling her she had found herself a good man. She knew now that it was true. And she could not let him go so easily.

"There was a witness," she said sadly, turning Edgar's ring on her finger. "A wolf named Lupus. But I doubt he would stand up in court and swear to what he saw. Father, I cannot go without a word to Edgar. I must stay until he returns."

"It is not gratitude he wants," Hugo reminded her.

"Gratitude is not what I intend to give him. I shall beg his forgiveness as humbly as I may. If, then, he still wishes to renounce the marriage vows then he must send me away himself. I shall not leave without seeing him."

For a long moment her father searched her face and what he saw there made him smile to himself. "You dreamed of a perfect knight, my love. I venture that you have found one — as perfect as any man may be. Very well, I cannot remove you by force. After all, you are still his wife."

Hugo and Ralf stayed in the dale for a few days with their escort of soldiers, but eventually they took leave of Lynette and set out for the long journey home The men-at-arms rode with them, in case Miles should chance another attack, and when they had gone Lynette wondered if she had made the right choice. Perhaps she should have bowed to fate and gone back to Braxby, but the thought of never seeing Edgar again was intolerable. She preferred to risk his anger, as long as she could speak with him at least once more.

July drifted by, with no sign of Edgar's return. As far as the valley people were concerned, life was normal. None of them knew the anxieties which plagued their young mistress beneath her outward show of calm good humour.

On the first of August, Lammastide, Ned took a sickle and with great ceremony cut the first stand of corn from his lord's fields. The grain was not properly ripe, but it was ground and made into a small loaf and the population gathered at the church for the Loaf Mass, to give thanks for the harvest which was now assured.

Everything seemed set fair and even the sun shone for days on end to ripen the corn to perfection, though for Lynette the heat was wearisome. She knew that people were beginning to murmur about the unusual length of Edgar's absence and they were disappointed that her slender figure showed no signs of thickening. At night she tossed beneath a single sheet, dreaming strange and frightening dreams, only to wake to yet another endless day of hoping and fearing.

Ned watched her with worried eyes, seeing how thin and pale she had grown. He kept assuring her that Edgar would return for the harvest celebration, but Lynette knew he could not be sure of it.

She began to fear that Edgar might never come home.

Suppose he and Miles had finally challenged each other. Suppose he was dead — but when this frantic fear came she consoled herself that someone would have brought the news. Instinct told her that Edgar still remained on the earth, but instinct could not inform her when he would return. The waiting stretched her nerves like the strings of a viol.

On a day when the heat lay over the valley like a thick blanket, she found herself snapping at Acha again — the poor child bore the brunt of her uneasiness and she was sorry for it.

"I am out of sorts," was her excuse. "Forgive me, Acha. It must be this dreadful heat. I am tempted to follow Sir Edgar's example and go for a swim."

"Oh, don't, my lady!" Acha gasped. "The goblin will pull you under!"

The thought of that pool of cool water lingered in Lynette's mind as she went about her work, and after dinner she ordered her horse to be saddled and set out accompanied by Frith. She told no one where she was going for fear they would try to stop her, but she needed to think and the heat seemed to cloud her brain. If she were cool for a while she might be able to plan the exact words to persuade Edgar to forgive her and let her prove how good a wife she could be.

Not a whisper of breeze stirred along the dale. The distances shimmered in a heat haze and by the river children in patched tunics paddled as they erected a tiny dam. Wilting in the heat, Lynette rode slowly, scarcely hearing the familiar sound of the watch-horn give its three reassuring notes.

Far down to the end of the valley she rode, where the oaks grew so close together that their branches formed a deep shade, only a few speckles of sunlight showing through. When she dismounted by the pool its rippling surface threw dancing reflections around the trees. She sank down onto one of the rocks, cupping her hands to splash water on her face, while Frith reached to lap from the pool.

Lynette took off her stockings and hitched up her skirts, slowly sliding her feet into the water. It felt wonderful, cooling her legs but making the rest of her feel even more sticky by contrast.

She glanced around at the silent trees. Seldom did anyone come to the pool and it was completely hidden from the track now that the woods had their full growth of leaves. Except where a small break in the canopy of branches allowed the sun to pour through, the place was sheltered from above, too, so no one on the hills could see her. And Edgar had no fear of swimming here.

Suddenly she wanted to share that experience with him. Shedding all her clothes, she tied her braids on top of her head before carefully letting herself down from the rock, her feet stretching for the bottom of the pool. It was deeper than she had expected and she found the water rising past her waist. Then her feet touched slippery rock and she was immersed to the ribs.

Keeping one hand firmly on the boulder above, she dipped in up to her chin, shivering deliciously as the water closed round her hot skin. How marvellous it felt to be cool all over after days of unbearable heat.

She laughed up at Frith, who stood on the edge of the pool regarding her enquiringly until she splashed water on him. He turned and bounded away, and then Lynette heard hoofbeats coming fast along the track, and a voice saying, "Frith? Here, boy!"

Edgar's voice! Relief and joy swooped through her, followed by dismay. Dear heaven, he must not discover her here, not like this.

Frantically, Lynette tried for a secure hold on the boulder to pull herself out of the pool, but it was too late for she glimpsed Edgar's black-clad figure striding through the trees towards her. She grabbed for her pile of clothes and sank back into the water clutching her chemise, which she hastily wrapped round her. It was not the best of cover for she had to hold it beneath her arms while at the same time clinging with one hand to a tuft of grass on the bank, and her feet slithered on the lichen-grown rock beneath her. How would Edgar greet her? Would he be angry? Oh, let him not be angry!

He appeared over the boulder, stepping up to stand there. Arms akimbo, he stared down at her with one black eyebrow lifted in a wicked hook.

"What have we here?" he said drily. "A watersprite? My lady, have a care. The goblin will get you."

Her face glowed with embarrassment. This was not the way she had planned to meet him, and she had not expected him to tease her. How typical of him to arrive unannounced and catch her at a disadvantage!

With every appearance of trying to be helpful, Edgar went down on one knee, extending his hand towards her. "Allow me, my lady."

"I can manage!" she gasped, aware that the thin chemise was in danger of floating away. "Go away, sir! Have you no decency?"

"Decency? My lady, you are the one who is naked."

"If you had given me the courtesy of some warning," Lynette said crossly, "I would have received you more suitably clad."

Edgar sat down cross-legged on the boulder, apparently prepared to stay there for ever, and regarded her with his dark head on one side.

"What could be more suitable to receive a husband after so long an absence? You make a most delightful picture, my lady, though I had not expected to find you here in the dale. Ned tells me your father came and has gone again, without you. Were you afraid that if you left my protection Sir Miles might capture you?"

"No, I — " She hesitated, for now that he was here she could think of no words to say. She took refuge in impatience. "If you were a gentleman you would go away and allow me to leave this pool and get dressed!"

Smiling wrily, he leaned on his knees so that his face was not far above hers. "As you have told me so often my lady, I am no gentleman, but a rude barbarian. Still, let me set your fears at rest — Sir Miles is gone to Normandy to await his little heiress. The king has told him not to return without permission."

"The king has?" she said blankly.

"Aye. My lord the good King Henry."

Lynette stared at him, wordless with amazement despite the shivers beginning to run through her.

"King William Rufus is dead," Edgar said gravely. "He was hit by an arrow while out hunting — an accident, I fear, or some say the judgment of God. The prince and I were in another part of the forest when it happened. Since the king died childless, his brother Prince Henry was the clear successor. He was crowned just three days later. Now he is busy arranging a marriage to the Saxon Princess Eadgyth, of the line of Alfred. It will please the Saxons, but also he loves her, after his fashion."

"I see," Lynette said faintly, trying to stop her teeth from chattering.

"So, since he is occupied in happy

matters, it was time for me to return to my lonely valley. I came with a heavy heart, my lady. Tell me, why did you not go with your father?"

"Because — because I wished to say — I wanted — "

"If you thank me," Edgar said steadily, "I may well give you a ducking."

The indignity of her situation, allied with this threat, made Lynette's temper rise. "You told me yourself that I would thank you some day! Edgar, let me out of this pool!"

"Wait!" he said, leaping to his feet. "I will bring something to wrap you in."

As he strode out of sight, Lynette reached up to the boulder and with an effort sprang clear of the water, scrambling to conceal her nakedness with the dripping shift. Her clothes were only a few feet away but she dared not reach for them or her scanty covering would slip. She sat shuddering as Edgar returned, bringing his wolfskin cloak, his gaze flicking over her bare limbs before he enveloped her in the cloak and helped her to her feet.

Shivering, she stood within the soft folds of his cloak, which covered her from chin to feet, her head tilted to look at her husband pleadingly.

"I want no thanks," he said, such hunger in his eyes that a flush crept from her toes to suffuse her entire body beneath the cloak.

"Then will you accept my apologies?" she asked in a small voice. "I am too proud, and too stubborn. My heart told me you were honourable, but I refused to listen to it. I have done you great wrong, since the day we met."

"You have." His voice was grave but the gleam in his eyes made her spirit leap in answer. "Is this why you stayed — to apologise?"

She felt as though she were drowning in the depths of dark eyes so full of tenderness that her insides felt molten. "My lord," she managed, "I am still your wife. If you wish me to leave you must yourself tell me so."

"I could never pronounce such words," Edgar said softly, reaching to untie her braids from round her head. "I have stayed away so long only because I feared the emptiness of my valley without you. When Ned said you were still here I could scarce contain myself. I sought you in a fever of hope and longing until Acha told me you had mentioned the pool."

With visibly trembling hands he began to unravel the ribbons that bound her hair. Soon it spilled over his cloak in a bright cloud. His fingers ran through the thick strands and he stared in wonder at the sight, lifting the shining locks to his lips. When his eyes met hers another shiver ran through her, but it was not caused by any chill. Her mouth began to ache for his kisses.

"If I make you pretty speeches," he murmured, "will you believe them?"

"My lord," she replied tremulously, "if you say the sky is green I will believe you."

"And if I ask you to stay here with me and fulfil your wedding vows?"

For answer she shook herself slightly and the cloak slipped, clinging briefly on her shoulders before falling in a heap at her feet. Edgar caught his breath as his gaze swept over her and he drew her closely into his arms, his eyes ablaze with desire. She felt the tremors that ran through his body and her own body responded with fire kindled deep inside her as his mouth took possession of hers.

He drew her down to lie beside him on the wolfskin cloak, lifting himself briefly to savour the sight of her, and even at that moment the devil of laughter danced in his eyes.

"My lady." His voice made it a caress. "Are you thinking now of Miles?"

"I know no Miles," she breathed, lifting her arms to tangle her fingers in his hair. "I know no man save Edgar of the Moor. My Saxon wizard. My lord. My love."

She drew his head down and kissed him softly at first, while his hands worked potent spells, drawing wild and mysterious feelings from untapped sources of her being. No longer were they Saxon and Norman, but lovers united in an abiding love, and Lynette learned the full wonder of his magic as the Black Saxon made her his true wedded wife.

THE END

WITH SOMEBODY ELSE
Theresa Charles

Rosamond sets off for Cornwall with Hugo to meet his family, blissfully unaware of the shocks in store for her.

A SUMMER FOR STRANGERS
Claire Hamilton

Because she had lost her job, her flat and she had no money, Tabitha agreed to pose as Adam's future wife although she believed the scheme to be deceitful and cruel.

VILLA OF SINGING WATER
Angela Petron

The disquieting incidents that occurred at the Vatican and the Colosseum did not trouble Jan at first, but then they became increasingly unpleasant and alarming.